ABOUT THE AUTHOR

Susan Grossey graduated from Cambridge University in 1987 and since then has made her living from crime. She spent twenty-five years advising financial institutions and others on money laundering – how to spot criminal money, and what to do about it – and has written many non-fiction books on the subject.

Her first work of fiction was the inaugural book in the Sam Plank series, *Fatal Forgery*, set in London in the 1820s and narrated by magistrates' constable Sam Plank. This was followed in the series by *The Man in the Canary Waistcoat*, *Worm in the Blossom*, *Portraits of Pretence*, *Faith, Hope and Trickery*, *Heir Apparent*, and *Notes of Change* which is the seventh (and final) book in the Sam Plank series.

Ostler is the first book in Susan's new series, the Cambridge Hardiman Mysteries. There will be four more books in this series, again set in the 1820s, but this time with Gregory Hardiman, a university constable in Cambridge, at the heart of them.

BY THE SAME AUTHOR

The Sam Plank Mysteries

Fatal Forgery
The Man in the Canary Waistcoat
Worm in the Blossom
Portraits of Pretence
Faith, Hope and Trickery
Heir Apparent
Notes of Change

Portraits of Pretence was given the "Book of the Year 2017" award by influential book review website Discovering Diamonds. And *Faith, Hope and Trickery* was shortlisted for the Selfies Award 2019.

The Solo Squid: How to Run a Happy One-Person Business

Susan in the City: The Cambridge News Years

OSTLER

Susan Grossey

Susan Grossey Publisher

This novel is a work of fiction. The events and characters in it, while based on real historical events and characters, are the work of the author's imagination.

Author contact details:

susangrosseyauthor@gmail.com

www.susangrossey.com

Sign up for my free monthly e-newsletter and receive your FREE complete e-book of *Fatal Forgery* (the first book in the Sam Plank Mysteries series)

www.susangrossey.com/insider-updates

Ostler / Susan Grossey -- 1st edition

ISBN 978-1-9160019-9-2

For Mary Burgess of the Cambridgeshire Collection

In thanks for her patience, curiosity and stubbornly cheerful assistance in the face of my daft questions

To her fair works did nature link
The human soul that through me ran;
And much it griev'd my heart to think
What man has made of man.

An extract from "Lines Written in Early Spring"
by William Wordsworth (1798)

Author's note

Any period of history has its own vocabulary, both standard and slang. The Regency was no different, and to capture the spirit of the time I have used words and phrases that may not be familiar to the modern reader. Moreover, Gregory is a Norfolk boy and sometimes uses words and phrases from his childhood. At the end of this book there is a glossary of these terms and their brief definitions. This glossary also contains an overview of the currency used at the time, and its equivalent modern spending power.

Chapter One

TEMPEST

With my eyes tightly closed, I pressed my hands and then my pillow against my ears. To blot out the horrors I conjured the image of my beloved Lucia and forced my lips to form the words. "She dwelt among the untrodden ways beside the springs of Dove, a maid whom there were none to praise and very few to love. A maid whom there were none to praise...." By now the clamour should be lessening but if anything it was growing, with cracks loud enough to wake the Devil and – even through my eyelids – the flash of muskets. And then I heard my name – a dying comrade perhaps – but surely no soldier was this polite, and with a woman's voice?

"Mr Hardiman, sir – are you awake?" The knocking at the door became more insistent. "Mr Hardiman, I am afeared for the roof."

I sat up and looked about me. My room, and my bed within it. There were no muskets and no dying comrades, but they would be back. As usual my nightshirt was damp with sweat and twisted around my legs.

"Mr Hardiman," I heard again. "The roof!"

"Calm yourself, Mrs Jacobs," I called back. "It is but a tempest."

I swung my legs out of bed, shivering as my feet touched the floorboards. I quickly shoved my feet into my slippers and reached for my coat, draping it around me before opening the door to my landlady. She was no older than I was, but the losses in her life had aged her. None of her four babies had thrived and it was a year since her husband had over-indulged at the Pickerel and fallen into the river on the way home, to be brought out lifeless the next morning on a waterman's hook. The long plait over her shoulder was shot through with grey, and the flame of the candle made the shadows under her eyes even more obvious.

"Will the roof hold, do you think?" she asked, looking upwards with a frown as the storm howled overhead. "It's creaking, and we've no neighbour on that side to protect us."

"I am sure it will, Mrs Jacobs," I said in the same tone as I used on nervous horses. "This is a new building – one of the sturdiest in Cambridge. And every English builder knows how to strengthen a roof against a winter tempest." We both jumped as thunder broke overhead and then glanced at each other.

"That was close," she said.

"Aye," I agreed. "We're right in the middle of it now, which means that it will soon pass."

"That's true," she said, and forced herself to a weak smile.

"I don't suppose it has woken Mr Carey," I said. "Not with his..." and I indicated my ear.

Mrs Jacobs shook her head. "Deaf as an adder, that one. But I shall not sleep again tonight. I may as well make a start on the day."

"Do you know the time?" I asked.

"Just gone four o'clock," she said, putting up a hand to shield her candle as she turned to go downstairs. "I heard the chimes a few minutes ago."

As I had promised Mrs Jacobs, the worse of the tempest had passed by the time I closed the front door behind me, but the wind was still strong. I turned my coat collar up and tucked my chin down as I walked along Jesus Lane. I had chosen my lodgings for several reasons, but chief amongst them was the location: on the edge of town, overlooking Butts Green and with the river in the distance, I could imagine myself once more in Norfolk, with the countryside stretching out around me. I might spend my working hours in the close confines of the town but at least once a day I needed to look out over wide green fields and stare up into empty skies. At this early hour I had the road to myself and I followed its gentle curve as it headed towards town. I crossed Bridge Street, which was deserted, and ducked into the passage leading to All Saints in the Jewry. The wind rattled the branches of the trees in the churchyard, and as I pushed open the gate leading into the yard of the Sun Hotel I could hear the stamping and snickering of the horses in their stalls. Horses do not like storms any more than Mrs Jacobs does; the thunder and lightning unsettles them, and I did not envy the coachmen and riders who would have to control them today. I walked over to the stables and put my head around the door, breathing in the warm smell of hay and animals.

"Good morning, ladies and gentlemen," I said softly. "The rain has passed and there'll be no more thunder or lightning, but there's still a strong wind blowing. An easterly."

When I was a lad I had taken plenty of ribbing for my habit of talking to our horses; my father had rolled his eyes and teased me that I was soft in the head. But a calm tone and gentle reassurance go a long way to quiet a frightened animal – be it horse or man – and they cost me nothing. Now if I expected an answer, well, that would be different.

I closed the stable door and walked across to the corner of the yard which led through into the kitchen. With the first coach of the day leaving at eight there would be passengers calling for their breakfast at seven and demanding cold meals to take on their journeys. Indeed I could hear someone moving around and I spied a flicker of light under the door. I knocked lightly and went in.

"Good morning, George," I said, looking through the steam for the familiar figure of the cook. "Did you hear that thunder in the night?"

"Who's that?" came a voice in reply. "That had better be you, Mr Ryder – of all the mornings to sleep in, when we've every bed taken and...". The person appearing round the corner was not the cook but rather William Bird, one of the proprietors of the Sun, and mine was plainly not the face he had hoped to see. "Ah, Hardiman," he said. "I don't suppose you've seen our cook, have you?" I shook my head. "Well, as you're early, you can set to work in here."

"The kitchen, sir?" I asked. "But I'm..."

"I know very well that you're an ostler," he interrupted, "but even an ostler knows how to heat water. Unless you'd rather go back to Jesus Lane to wake Mrs Bird and tell her the cook's gone missing?" I shook my head again. "I thought not."

By the time the bell of the Round Church tolled ten I was more than ready for my noonday meal, with two hours still to wait. I lifted my arm in farewell as the *Telegraph* pulled out of the yard, the horses skittish and whinnying, and rolled my head from side to side to release the stiffness in my neck. Another unwelcome souvenir from Boney. As I stood in the yard, my breath clouding in front of me, one of the scullery maids trotted past, her arms full of bedding.

"The missus says you're to go in for a hot drink when you've checked the stables," she said, looking at me and then glancing away quickly. I could only imagine what she and the other young girls said about my face.

"Thank you," I said. "Any sign of Mr Ryder?"

"Not a whisper," she called over her shoulder as she headed for the laundry room, "so I don't fancy our chances of a decent meal."

As any soldier will tell you, there's a world of difference between activity and chaos. From first thing in the morning until last thing at night, the kitchen of the Sun was busy, feeding travellers and coachmen and – in between our duties around the inn – the workers. But George Ryder knew what he was doing: with his apron straining across his ample stomach and a red kerchief – always red – hanging loose about his neck, its ends used to mop the sweat from his face, he was the still centre of that kitchen. Without him, as it was today, it was simply a swirling mess – a maelstrom, if you will – of movement to no organised end. Maelstrom is one of my new words – I like the unexpected order of the letters.

I stood quietly to one side and watched the innkeeper's wife. Mrs Bird's airs and graces made her unpopular with most of the staff at the inn. She usually kept herself to the public areas, welcoming travellers and dealing with the great and the good who sometimes used our premises for their auctions and their meetings. Today, however, she found herself standing in for Mr Ryder, and she was a poor substitute. Ordinarily she was well turned out but today she had cut short her toilette: a scullery maid's apron had been pinned crookedly over her dress, and her hair was shoved up under a cap, with a few strands falling loose to stick to her rosy face. She stood in the middle of the kitchen, hands on hips, and shouted at anyone within range. For the most part, whoever it was simply said, "Yes, ma'am," and then carried on as they had been.

But huddled over the largest sink, his shoulders quivering, was Poor Jamie, the simpleton hired to wash pots. George Ryder had known Jamie's grandfather and his father and had taken on the lad out of sympathy for them: the whole family was always down at heel but as honest as the day is long, and that's a rare quality these days. The cook just left Poor Jamie to it, to let him whistle little tunes to himself as he washed pot after pot, and we all knew that any change in the lad's routine would upset him. I waited until Mrs Bird's attention was elsewhere and walked over to the sink.

"Hello, Jamie," I said quietly. He quickly looked up at me and then back down at his sink. I put a calming hand on his shoulder and could feel his bones as he trembled. "A bit of a racket in here today," I continued. "You'll be missing Mr Ryder."

Jamie nodded and scrubbed at a dish. "I told him he'd be in trouble, Mr Hardiman," he said, his eyes darting to my face and away again. "I told him."

"Did you?" I said. He nodded. "You told Mr Ryder he'd be in trouble?" Another nod. "When did you tell him this?" I asked.

"Last night," said Jamie, lifting the dish from the water and leaning across to stack it on the board.

"And what made you think he'd be in trouble?" I asked.

"The men," said the lad, plunging his hands into the water again. "The men he went home with." He looked up at me, sadness on his face. "Bad men. I don't like them."

"Bad men?" repeated William Bird distractedly, as he paged backwards and forwards through the ledger on his desk. "That's not much to go on, is it? And you can't put much store by what Poor Jamie says – the lad's a noddy."

"But even a noddy can see things," I replied. "And he's very fond of George – of Mr Ryder. He probably knows more about Mr Ryder's routine than we do."

The innkeeper gave a small shrug. "Perhaps," he allowed.

"The Wisbech coach is not due to leave for another two hours," I said. "I could call round to Mr Ryder's lodging. He might be laid up with the ague." As I said it, I knew it was unlikely: even a sick man would be able to send a message.

"The horses?" asked Bird, pausing to look up at me.

"All taken care of," I confirmed.

"Go – go then," he said, waving his arm impatiently. "Find the blasted man. If my wife has to stay in that kitchen for the afternoon, my life won't be worth living."

Chapter Two

Horsemen

Unlike me, George Ryder was Cambridge born and bred. I had chosen to live on the edge of town, for reasons I have already explained to you, but George and his family lived where the Ryders have always lived: the crowded, jostling, noisy and, to be frank, filthy turmoil of the Castle End. Once upon a time the area around the castle had been the fancy part of town, but when the soldiers left and the scholars arrived, all the money trickled down the hill. Left behind was a jumble of dwellings, many of them little more than hovels, huddled around three churches. Reluctant to leave familiar streets but with earnings from the Sun, George Ryder had managed to move his wife, their five children, his parents and his mother-in-law from rooms overlooking an airless courtyard into a tiny but spotless house near Pound Hill. His wife brought in a little extra money by selling pasties to the crowds on market days, and on other days they all enjoyed the open space on Pound Green.

I waited for a cart to clear the Great Bridge before I walked over it – as you may have observed yourself, horses can be alarmed by the way the walls of the bridge close in on them, and you do not want to be trapped alongside a frightened horse. Glancing down at the river I saw two watermen shouting at each other; it seemed that one of them had craftily taken the berth at the wharf that the other had intended. Magdalene Street was quiet: at this hour, members of the University would be about their business, not returning to their colleges until midday – which the clock of St Giles told me was still more than an hour off.

I started up the hill and then turned left into St Peter's Lane. When I reached the green, I barely had time to look for Ryder's house before a woman coming out of her front door spotted me.

"Mr Hardiman, isn't it?" she said, pulling her shawl around her against the chill wind that was whipping around.

"Mrs Ryder," I replied, dipping my head in greeting. "It is indeed: once seen, never forgotten." I felt my hand lift towards my damaged face and forced it into my pocket instead. The cook's wife was as slender as he was round, which is a pairing I have often observed. For myself, I prefer a woman with a bit more softness to her – but that is of no interest to you, I am sure. Mrs Ryder wore no finery or decoration – her husband's wages would not stretch that far – but her clothes were neat, tidy and clean. A trim little maw, my mother would have called her.

"I was just walking into town," she said. She stopped, suddenly uncertain. "Will you come inside, Mr Hardiman?"

"Were you coming to tell us that Mr Ryder is unwell?" I asked. She looked puzzled.

"Unwell?" she repeated. "He is not at the Sun?" I shook my head. "Then where is he, Mr Hardiman?" she asked.

Poor Jamie stood in the doorway of Mr Bird's room, shoulders hunched, hands clasped together, looking down at the ground but stealing little glances at each of us, like a nervous dog.

"For pity's sake, lad," said Bird, "it's not a hard question, is it?"

Jamie bowed his head even more and said nothing.

"If I may," I said to the innkeeper. He threw his hands in the air and turned to look out of the window into Trinity Street.

"Jamie," I said softly. "You're not in trouble, but Mr Ryder needs your help. He's helped you before, hasn't he?" The lad looked up at me and nodded. "And now he needs you to help him. It's what friends do, isn't it – we help each other."

Another nod. "My ma says I'm a big help," he whispered.

"Good lad," I said. "Your ma is right. Now, this is Mr Ryder's wife." I indicated Mrs Ryder, sitting pale as a dove on the chair by the desk.

"I know," said Jamie. "I seed them once in town." He looked at Mrs Ryder and pointed to his own head. "She wore a green hat. With a flower."

Mrs Ryder smiled weakly. "I did," she agreed. "My church hat. George – Mr Ryder – tells me that you're the best pot-washer he's ever had, Jamie."

Jamie flushed with pleasure.

"Now, Jamie," I continued. "Mr Ryder didn't go home last night and you know he hasn't come to the kitchen today, and Mrs Ryder is worried about him. Your ma would be worried if you didn't go home, wouldn't she?" Jamie nodded vigorously. "You told me that you saw him yesterday evening, with some bad men, didn't you?" I continued. Jamie nodded again. "Now, if I could talk to these men, I could find out where Mr Ryder is, and then Mrs Ryder can stop worrying. Can you tell me what they looked like?"

"If I tell you," said Jamie, "Mrs Ryder can stop worrying."

"That's it, lad," I said.

Despite himself, Bird turned from the window to listen. Ryder was a good cook and the innkeeper was damned if he was going to lose him to the competition. He'd once caught Thomas Mitchell from the Eagle talking to Ryder in the kitchen, and we all knew that if anywhere in Cambridge needed a good cook it was the Eagle.

"There was three of them," said Jamie. He glanced at the notebook in my hand. Like many who cannot read or write, he both revered and feared the written word.

"I've a terrible memory these days, Jamie," I said with a smile. "I'm just writing down what you say so I don't forget. You've seen me writing things down before. I can show you – here." I turned the notebook so that he could see the marks on the page. "See: that's your name there, with the big hook at the beginning – that says Jamie." I pointed with my pencil.

He peered at the notebook, then nodded and continued. "They were all tall. Taller'n me. Strong. With dark hair."

"All three of them? They looked alike?" I asked. Jamie nodded. "Brothers, do you think?"

"Oh, aye," Jamie said. "The Greenway brothers. Bad men, my ma says."

Bird thumped his desk. "Good heavens, lad! If you knew who they were, why didn't you say?"

Jamie looked stricken and his eyes darted from me to Mrs Ryder and back again. "Mr Hardiman asked me to tell him what they looked like – he didn't ask what they were called."

Mrs Ryder reached up and put her hand on Jamie's bony wrist. "Don't you worry, Jamie. You've been a good boy – a great help, like your ma says – and when I see Mr Ryder I shall tell him so."

After Jamie had gone back to the kitchen, we sent Mrs Ryder home. She said that George had never mentioned anyone called Greenway, but that he did not often discuss his work at home – with such a busy household, there were plenty of other things to talk about. I promised to send word as soon as we knew anything, and she said she would likewise send word if her husband turned up.

I turned to the innkeeper. "D'you know these men?" I asked.

He shook his head. "I've heard the name mentioned, I think. You?"

"Sadly, yes," I said. "The two younger ones are just bullies – handy with their fists – but the oldest, well, he's nasty with it. Jem."

"Did you meet them through George?" asked Bird.

"We've never been introduced, as such," I said. "But you can't be as free with your punches as they are without people noticing." The innkeeper raised an eyebrow at me but said nothing. A smart man knows when not to ask. "I'll have a word with the other horsemen around town," I said.

The horsemen. That's what we call ourselves, the ostlers. Any fool can look after dogs or oxen or sheep; those beasts think mainly of their stomachs and are happy to do whatever a man tells them in exchange for a full belly. But horses are different, you know it yourself, and it takes a different sort of man to look after them. A groom will live with the same animals for years, learning their ways and earning their trust. But ostlers, well, we have to take what we're given. A coach comes in with a pair or four, and they might be mild or wild. They're always tired, of course – sweating and steaming. They might have thrown a shoe, needing a visit from the farrier, or want liniment for a strained muscle or salve for raw skin – none of which puts them in good humour. They're hungry and thirsty and impatient to be out of harness and resting on soft hay in the stall. They might be sick of the sight of the animal they have worked alongside all day, or unable to settle without that familiar companion. And all of this the ostler is expected to understand within minutes of meeting each horse. Some take on the job for money, but if that's your reason, you'll not stick it for long, I can tell you. You have to do it for the horses.

It's probably right that I'm a horseman, because when I was a lad my father called me his horse-boy. We had three horses back then, Suffolk Sorrels, with their bright chestnut coats, sturdy legs and strong shoulders, built for working all day in the heavy clay soil. Just like us, my father used to say: Hardiman by name and hardy man by nature. I remember the three – Red, Lark and Penny – for their gentle souls and their determination: at a word from the driver, they would heave forward into the harness and almost throw themselves onto their knees in their determination to please him. When I turned thirteen, more often than not that driver would be me. There were any number of tasks on the farm that my father could have given me but he saw that I was happiest with the horses, and they with me. Not that he was a sentimental man – far from it – but a wise farmer knows that he'll get more work from content animals, be they horses or children.

I'm sure the same thought was in the mind of Major Howard – Captain Howard as he was then – when he saw me talking to the horses on our ship as we rolled and clawed our way across the Bay of Biscay. At least a man can understand what the sea is, but all a horse knows is that the wood beneath his hooves is rising and falling and that the air is full of sharp smells and sounds of alarm. To distract myself from what lay ahead, I ducked under the railing of the stalls and moved slowly between the tightly-packed animals, running my hands gently along their flanks and making low reassurances. I had identified the horse being watched by all the others and made my way to him. His ears flicked to follow my progress and once I was alongside him I took care to move where he could see me. His glistening eyes turned to me and he blew out heavily before taking in a deep scent of me; I made sure I was clear of his hooves as he adjusted his position to make room for me. I raised my hand carefully and made a steady, calming stroke down his shoulder. I could feel his muscles tremble under my touch. I repeated the movement perhaps a dozen times, murmuring nonsense to him all the while. The animal's head gradually lowered and his eyelids closed, just for a moment. Around him, the other horses took their lead from him and quieted. I stood silently and rested my cheek against his shoulder, feeling his warmth and smelling the tang of his sweat.

"A horseman, eh?" said a quiet voice.

I looked round slowly and there was Captain William Howard.

"Yes, sir," I said. "Well, no, not officially. But at home I cared for horses."

"Then I'd be a fool to put you to work anywhere but the stable," he said. And indeed, from the moment we set foot ashore, I spent more time with horses than with soldiers. And when it was over and I could return to England, and my father was long-gone and the farm with him, and I craved the anonymity of a town where no-one knew me, it was still horses that drew me, and the men who worked with them.

Most ostlers live in, tucked away in their ostries alongside or above the stables, surrounded by the scent and sound and warmth of the horses. And it was in his snug loft at the Eagle that I found Arthur Milton. Older than me by perhaps ten years, Arthur had spent his whole life in Cambridge – he knew the ways of the town, and had a keen nose for trouble.

"The Greenway boys?" he said, shaking his head. "I'm sorry for George if he's on the wrong side of them. Fine cook too. I've heard you eat well at the Sun." He reached over to a low table and picked up a covered plate; he lifted the cloth and inspected the food with disappointment.

"Aye, we do," I agreed. "But you've heard nothing about George?"

"Now I didn't say that, did I?" he said with a half-smile, covering the plate again and putting it on the floor. He leaned forward and spoke more quietly. "One of the brothers – Sam – was in here the night before last, half seas over, and yelping about some fellow who owed them money. The brothers had come by some meat for him and he was complaining that it wasn't good enough and refusing to pay." He sat back. "Could be George – could be someone else. But Jem Greenway is not the most patient of creditors."

"The last anyone saw of George Ryder was last night," I said, half to myself. "Poor Jamie saw him leave the Sun with the Greenways."

"All three of them?" asked Arthur.

"That's what Jamie said," I replied.

"He's a simpleton but he's no liar," said Arthur. "Takes a bit of brains to cook up a lie. If that's what Jamie said, that's what he saw. And I'm sorry to hear it."

"What do you mean?" I asked.

"Well," said Arthur, "if George had been with just Jem, or even two of them, he might have had a chance to get away. He might be lying low somewhere. But if the three of them took him – well, I'm sorry to hear it is all I'm saying."

Arthur's words went round in my head as I walked briskly back to the Sun – and I was only just in time: the *Wisbech Day* was coming towards me down Trinity Street. I ducked quickly into the yard, ready to grab the harness as soon as the driver gave the signal.

"Only just made it through," he said as he stowed his whip and then climbed down from the box. His long coat and tall hat served to keep most of him warm as he travelled but his face was ruddy with cold and he stamped on the spot to bring some feeling back into his booted feet.

"An accident on the Huntingdon road?" I asked, my hands working at releasing the animals from their traces.

"No," he replied. "A crowd blocking Great Bridge. They've found a body in the water." And he set off purposefully in the direction of the privy.

Chapter Three

INQUEST

Three days later Mrs Ryder and I went to the inquest for her husband. I met her outside the Hoop; her eyes were hollow, with smudges of sleeplessness below them, and she looked uneasy wearing her green church hat on a Monday. I saw her glance at my coat and was glad that I had thought to brush off my boots. Coroners often held their inquests in the Hoop, as it had one of the largest and cleanest assembly rooms in Cambridge. I knew John Ingle by reputation, of course: he was an important man in town, acting as solicitor for two or three of the colleges and for the University itself as well as serving as coroner. And I knew that he rode a fine bay mare called Duchess and treated her with great gentleness. But this was the first time that I had seen him.

Mrs Ryder and I entered the room being used for the inquest. There were – I quickly counted – fourteen chairs for the jury, flanked seven either side of the coroner, with other seats pressed into service for the public. I had explained to Mrs Ryder the purpose of the inquest as best I understood it, and warned her that her husband's body would be in the room. She was admirably controlled: I heard a very slight intake of breath as she looked at the shape under the cloth on the table and then she sat neatly on a wooden stool, tucking her legs to one side and clasping her hands in her lap.

"Would you prefer a more comfortable seat?" I asked quietly. "Something with a back to it?" She shook her head. I stood behind her, against the wall. I had had a word with the clerk and was thankful to learn that the jury had already been sworn in, as this meant that the viewing of the body had taken place earlier and Mrs Ryder would not have to endure that. Although it was a cold day the fire had not been lit; with one dead body and more than two dozen living ones to be in the room, it seemed a wise decision. There room was already fairly busy and more people arrived every minute, some greeting acquaintances while others stood alone, and the members of the jury took their seats.

Almost the last person to enter the room was a stocky, rather shifty looking man, wearing the cloth cap, bright neckerchief and blue serge apron of a fishmonger. As he took off his cap, he glanced over and caught sight of Mrs Ryder. She sat even more upright. They stared at each other for a long moment and then he dropped his gaze and shuffled behind another man.

As the tall clock struck ten, the door opened again and everyone who was sitting rose to their feet as the coroner made his way to his chair at the head of the table. John Ingle had obviously been a handsome man; his face was open and kind, with a strong nose and bright eyes. He had a good head of curled white hair, which I guessed from his colouring had once been blonde. Surprisingly, given the company he must keep, he had not run to fat, and in his early sixties he still had a trim figure – perhaps those hours in the saddle visiting outlying villages were a blessing as well as a duty.

The coroner pulled out his chair, nodded and everyone sat. The clerk of the court – a pale, spare young man in a coat at least one size too large for him – handed his sheaf of papers to the coroner. Mr Ingle put a pair of spectacles on his nose and read aloud.

"The jury having been sworn in, I shall now open this inquest into the death of Mr George Ryder, whose body was taken from the river by the Great Bridge on Friday last. I call the surgeon Mr Newsome."

A young man with his dark hair brushed forward in the Continental style stood up and bowed to the coroner and the jury. He wore sombre dark clothes and a tall white collar with a spotless neckcloth. "I am Daniel Newsome, surgeon," he said. "May I consult my notes, sir?" The coroner nodded and Newsome stooped to retrieve a black-covered book from the satchel leaning against the leg of his chair. He turned to a page marked with a slip of paper and read aloud in a clear voice. "I was called to attend the deceased on Friday last, at about one o'clock. He had been pulled from the river and life was recently extinct."

The coroner held up his hand and the surgeon halted. "How can you be sure that the death was recent?" asked the coroner.

The surgeon stepped forward, put his notebook on the table and with two hands took hold of the cloth covering the body. "May I?" he asked. The coroner nodded and Newsome carefully, delicately folded back the cloth so that the corpse was exposed to chest level. I put my hand on Mrs Ryder's shoulder and felt her stiffen. Newsome pointed to the face of the corpse. "You see here," he said, "that the face is still recognisable. There is very little bloating to the fleshy parts of the head, or to the hands." He reached for the cloth again and turned it down further, tucking it carefully under the arm of the body. "A body that is submerged in water for anything more than a day would show significant signs of bloating." He consulted his notebook again. "You will see that there are marks on the lower arm and hand – these are present on the other arm as well. Bodies pulled from water often exhibit marks like these, from hitting underwater obstacles or the riverbed – grazes, rough cuts and the like. But upon examining the marks more closely, I consider that they were made before the body entered the water. The positioning of them is wrong for underwater damage."

"Please explain, Mr Newsome," said the coroner.

"If a dead body is in the water," said the surgeon, "it will generally float face downwards, with the arms and legs submerged. The hands will curl over, and the knuckles will take the impact of any grazes or knocks." He hunched his shoulders and bent his arms to illustrate the point. "But if the marks – as they are on Mr Ryder – are predominantly on the underside of the lower arms and the palms of the hands, this suggests that they were acquired while he was defending himself." Now the surgeon raised his arms above his head.

"I see," said Ingle, nodding and making a note. "To be clear, Mr Newsome: your opinion is that the injuries were sustained before Mr Ryder entered the water, and that they are consistent with fending off an attack?"

Newsome did not answer immediately; he was preoccupied with gently covering the body once again by pulling the sheet up to the man's neck. I was impressed by the care and solicitude he showed to a man who was beyond appreciating it. When he had finished, he looked at the coroner. "It is, sir, yes," he confirmed.

"And the large bruise on the forehead?" asked the coroner, pointing.

"That is what I believe Mr Ryder was trying to fend off," said Newsome. "I have examined it closely and am of the view that it was caused by a cudgel of some sort – wooden, I should imagine. You can see that the skin is broken but not as much as it would have been had the weapon been a stone, or a metal implement."

Ingle held up his hand again. "You used the word 'weapon', Mr Newsome," he said. "Could not the bruise on the head be accidental? Perhaps Mr Ryder tripped, hit his head, lost sense and then fell into the river?"

Newsome shook his head. "If a man tripped and hit his head hard enough to cause that injury in that location, there would be other damage to his face – most likely a broken nose," he said, "and there is no such damage. However, I do think it highly likely that Mr Ryder lost sense, and hope that this gives his widow some comfort: he would have died quickly and peacefully once in the water." He looked across at Mrs Ryder and she gave one quick, controlled nod of her head.

"Are you of the view, Mr Newsome," asked Ingle with a dash of impatience, "that Mr Ryder died by drowning? That he was alive when he entered the water?"

"Yes, sir," replied the surgeon. "In my opinion, given the state of the body when pulled from the water, the location of the marks on the arms and hands and the type of injury on the head, Mr Ryder was attacked, tried to defend himself, received a final blow which rendered him senseless, and then fell into or was thrown into the river, where he drowned."

"Thank you, Mr Newsome," said the coroner.

The surgeon bowed once more, retrieved his notebook and returned to his seat.

Two witnesses were then called; both were watermen who worked on the river. John Bartholomew confirmed that he had seen the body caught in the weeds under the Great Bridge, and George Smith confirmed that he had helped his friend to pull the body clear and steer it to the bank with their boat-hooks.

"And at what time was this – your first sighting of the body?" asked Ingle.

"Noon," said Bartholomew confidently. "Just heard the bells." Smith nodded in agreement. And given that the driver of the Wisbech coach had seen the commotion and told me of it when he arrived at the inn, I knew that they were right.

"And can you confirm what the surgeon has told us – that there was very little bloating to the body? Swelling – puffed up?"

The two men both shook their heads. "I seen plenty of drowned bodies, your honour – your lord – sir," said Bartholomew, who was clearly the spokesman of the pair. "I been a waterman since I was a nipper, and before that went on my pa's boat – seen plenty of them in the water. And this one was fresher than most." He glanced over at Mrs Ryder. "Sorry, missus."

"Thank you, Mr Bartholomew, Mr Smith," said the coroner. "Having heard all the evidence, the jury will now consider its verdict."

The fourteen men of the jury stood and with a little difficulty, given the amount of furniture in the room, gathered in a huddle by the window. The coroner stood near them but not among them, ready to assist them with understanding the evidence they had heard should he be needed. In the event they managed without him, and after only a few minutes the foreman of the jury walked across to the coroner and spoke quietly to him. Ingle nodded, and in his turn beckoned to the clerk and spoke quietly to him. The jury took their seats once more and when the room had settled the foreman rose to his feet.

"Having heard evidence concerning the death of Mr George Ryder," he said, "we the jury return an open verdict." He bowed his head to the coroner and sat down.

Mrs Ryder looked up at me in confusion. Perhaps catching her movement, the coroner spoke. "An open verdict means that we acknowledge a crime but are as yet unable to name the criminal. This inquest can be reopened at any later date should further evidence come to light. The body will be conveyed to Addenbrooke's Hospital to allow the surgeon to perform a more detailed post mortem examination, and will then be released for burial the day after tomorrow. Thank you gentlemen – our business for today is concluded."

The door was opened and a few people left – among them, the fishmonger – before the rest of the throng parted to allow the coroner and then the jury to leave. I placed my hand lightly on Mrs Ryder's shoulder to tell her to stay seated until the room had cleared; there was no need for her to be jostled or rushed. When she and I were the only people left in the room, the door opened and two men came in carrying a long, broad plank. They stopped short when they saw us.

"Beg pardon, sir," said one of them. "We're to take..." He nodded towards the body hidden once again under the cloth. "We've a cart outside, to go to the hospital."

Mrs Ryder stood up. She walked silently to the table and gazed down at the covered body. She reached for the cloth and the porter who had spoken made a movement towards her but I put out my hand to stop him. Mrs Ryder carefully lifted the cloth that was covering her husband's right arm. She took hold of his hand in both of hers and then bent to kiss it before covering it once again. She nodded her thanks to the porters and the second, silent one held the door open for us as we left the room.

Once we were outside in the street, Mrs Ryder let her shoulders drop. There was a cutting wind blowing along the street and she pulled her shawl tighter about her.

"Shall I walk you home, Mrs Ryder?" I asked.

She shook her head. "'Tis kind of you, sir, but a few minutes to myself is what I need. They'll be waiting for me at home, to know what's happened, and I shall have to tell them. A post mor..."

"Post mortem examination," I supplied.

She nodded. "That means they'll cut him up, doesn't it?"

"It's a close examination, yes," I agreed. "But done with respect, by a proper surgeon."

"I can't tell his parents that, or the youngsters," she said decisively. "I'll tell them he's gone to be fitted and dressed for his coffin. They'll understand that." She suddenly looked up at me, uncertainty on her face for the first time. "The open verdict – a crime but no criminal. Should I tell them that, d'ye think? Or bear it alone?"

"You're not alone, Mrs Ryder," I said. "George was well-liked at the Sun, and I am sure his friends will not see you struggle. But I know that is not what you mean." She shook her head. "My advice," I continued, "would be to let your family think that George died in an accident – that he slipped on the ice, hit his head and tumbled into the river." I sighed. "I'm not one for an untruth, Mrs Ryder, but it is hard to see what good it would do them to think otherwise. Meanwhile, I give you my word that we will find whoever is really responsible for George's death."

It was not an entirely selfless offer. I had liked George Ryder, and I felt sorry for his widow, but more than that I needed something to occupy my mind. I did not want to have time to dwell on those things that troubled me – I knew only too well where that could lead.

Mrs Ryder looked up at me. "I am grateful, Mr Hardiman," she said.

I nodded. "And to that end, Mrs Ryder," I said, turning my own coat collar up against the wind, "the fishmonger up there." I jerked my head to indicate the room upstairs. "Who was he?"

"George's brother," she said, the distaste evident in her voice. "William – Bill, he's called. Always on the sniff for an easy way to make money, that one. Afeared of hard work, George said. We kept our distance – or at least I did." She shrugged. "But you know brothers – I think George did see him from time to time. Probably slipped him a few shillings too. He was soft-hearted, my George. More's the pity." She reached up and wiped away a tear.

"I disagree, Mrs Ryder," I said. "It's never a pity if someone is soft-hearted. There's not enough of it in the world, in my opinion."

Chapter Four

Market

The next morning I waited until the *Tally Ho* had left for Royston and onwards to London, the driver cursing the foul weather, and stuck my head into the kitchen to tell the cook that I was heading out for an hour. Mr Bullen at the Hoop had lent us his apprentice cook for a few days until we could find a replacement for Mr Ryder, and the poor fellow was certainly learning quickly about life as head cook in a busy coaching inn. As I turned to go he shouted after me.

"Are you going anywhere near the market?" he called, lifting an arm to wipe the sweat from his forehead.

"I am," I said, walking back towards him.

"We have no butter left," he said, "or at least, not that I can find. Can you buy me half a yard, no, better make that three-quarters. You have the money?"

"I do," I said. "Three-quarters of a yard. I'll be back in an hour."

The cook turned to snatch a boiling pan from the stove and yelped as the water splashed his hand. I beat a hasty retreat.

I walked along Trinity Street, stepping to one side to allow a gentleman on a handsome black horse to pass, and turned into Market Street. I could hear the clock of Great St Mary's tolling the hour when I walked into the Butter Market. I decided to run the cook's errand before my own; I certainly did not want to be responsible for the poor man trying to prepare midday meals without butter. I found the butter seller favoured by Mrs Jacobs as I had never had reason to complain about the quality of the butter at my lodgings. Glancing at my face and then away again, as those who meet me for the first time are wont to do, he bent down to his butter basket and pulled out a new length of butter. He cut it into quarters and wrapped three of them in a cloth and handed them to me, holding up his fingers to indicate the price. I paid and thanked him and put the butter carefully into my satchel. I then turned my thoughts to my own reason for coming to the market.

I made my way to the conduit and walked up the middle of the market. There was the usual cacophony of cries. I do like that word – it sounds of what it is. Stall-holders called to buyers to examine their wares, see how fresh, brought in only this morning, the tastiest in the land! Butter, of course, and meat, poultry, fruit, vegetables, milk, herbs: no matter how ambitious the cook or fussy the diner, they would find whatever they wanted in Cambridge market. And with the market toll now at a penny a day for each stall, no-one wanted to go home with anything but an empty cart or barrow. I shook my head at them all and carried on into Peas Hill. Here the market narrowed, with fish barrows crowding towards the middle of the lane. Thankfully the cold weather kept the air clear, but in the height of summer a visit to Peas Hill could be a pungent experience. Of course it is no hill, but it is slightly elevated and so the water and guts from the barrows and stalls can run off. Again, there was a handsome choice on offer, from salmon to Colchester oysters, as well as mackerel, herring (my own particular favourite), sprats, eels and jacks. But I was looking at the sellers rather than their fish. And about halfway along I saw him, reaching across his barrow to turn his display to better advantage: Bill Ryder. I stopped in front of him.

"Mr Ryder," I said.

He looked up with a smile that quickly fell from his face.

"You were with Mary, at the inquest," he stated.

"I was," I said. "Some might think it odd that a man would not comfort his brother's widow at such a time."

He stood more upright and crossed his arms. "And some might think that it's none of your business, Mr...?"

"Gregory Hardiman," I supplied. "I work at the Sun." Ryder's shoulders dropped and he uncrossed his arms. "Why: who did you think I might be?" I asked. "One of your creditors?"

"So Mary's been telling tales," he said unpleasantly.

"Mrs Ryder wants to know why her husband was murdered," I said. I saw no reason to spare this man's feelings. "I should think that would concern you too, as a loving brother."

He had the good grace to look ashamed. "Look," he said, "there's too many flapping ears around here." The woman examining the fish at the next barrow looked outraged and stalked off. "I'll come to the Sun later – at five o'clock."

I shook my head. "The yard is too busy then. It will have to be four o'clock." Ryder nodded. "I'll be in the stables," I said. "Don't make me come looking for you, Mr Ryder."

The *Bury* had just pulled out of the yard when I saw Bill Ryder slip through the gate. Even without hearing Mary Ryder's comments at the inquest, I would have taken him for a shifty fellow. His glance darted around while he kept close to the wall, his shoulders slightly hunched as though to make himself less visible – a smaller target, as we used to say in the army. The mischief in me made me hail him all the more loudly for it.

"Mr Ryder," I called across the yard. "Over here."

He looked startled and made his way around the edge of the yard to meet me.

"Mr Hardiman," he said. "Four o'clock, as agreed."

"Two minutes past, Mr Ryder," I said. "The driver of the *Bury* prides himself on leaving the yard to the sound of the bell, and he's halfway along St Andrew's Street by now." I stood to one side and indicated that he should go ahead of me into the stables. "After you: we'll head upstairs where it's warm." We walked through the stables, and out of habit I made sure that all the doors were shut, trying each one as I passed it. There were three horses staying overnight, their owners breaking their journeys in Cambridge, and they whinnied quietly as they settled into their new surroundings. At the rear of the stables was a ladder leading up into the loft. Under the eaves was space for a bed, should an ostler want to live in, while two rickety chairs, made more comfortable by the addition of cushions that had seen better days in the Sun's parlour, were positioned in the tallest part of the room. Between them, an upturned crate served as a table. In honour of my guest, I had brought a pot of coffee from the kitchen and wrapped a cloth around it to keep it warm. To my mind, there are few smells as comforting as that of coffee mixed with the aroma of warm hay and horses. I sat in one of the chairs and, without asking, unwrapped the pot, poured two cups of coffee and handed one to Ryder. He stooped to take it from me and then sat down.

He sipped his coffee and looked up at me, surprised. "This is good," he said. "Not too bitter."

"One of your brother's innovations," I said. The fishmonger raised an eyebrow. "It means a new idea, a change," I explained. "I like words – finding the right one." He said nothing but took another sip. I continued. "It costs a little more, the coffee, but if people like it they order it again." I took a sip myself. "He buys it... he bought it from a coffee dealer on Willow Walk, but kept his exact source secret." I shook my head. "I hope he told someone." I looked questioningly at Ryder.

"Ha!" he said. "Saint George wouldn't have told me, if that's what you're thinking."

"No love lost between you, then," I said. "I thought as much, from what his wife – his widow – said."

"Mary never liked me," he said, looking around the loft. I waited, drinking my coffee. "Kept George on a tight rein, that one. On the straight and narrow." He glanced back at me, and I thought I glimpsed a wetness in his eyes before he looked down at his cup again. "It's not right, what happened to him."

"Slipping in the dark, you mean?" I asked. "Falling in the river?"

Bill Ryder gave me a long look. "You know as well as I do, Mr Hardiman, that there was no slipping and falling. It's like the coroner said: a crime without a criminal."

I shook my head. "Not quite, Mr Ryder. There certainly is a criminal – we just don't know who he is. Or who they are."

Ryder looked up at me and then quickly dropped his gaze again.

"The thing is, Mr Ryder," I said, putting my cup down on the crate and leaning back in my chair, "I think you know more than you've said. Shall I tell you what I think happened?"

Ryder said nothing but shrugged his shoulders.

"I think that your brother found himself on the wrong side of the Greenway brothers," I started. "From what I hear about them, they are not patient men, and I think they like to take care of their own justice if they think someone has wronged them. Perhaps they didn't mean to kill him, perhaps they meant only to beat him as a warning – but kill him they did. And I think their warning has reached the right ears, hasn't it, Mr Ryder? I think it has reached your ears and stopped your mouth." I shook my head. "I would not be you for all the riches in the world, Mr Ryder. With that on my conscience. With wishes the past to undo." He looked at me, frowning slightly. "Wordsworth," I explained. Another frown. "The poet."

"Do I look like I have time to read poetry?" asked Ryder.

Now it was my turn to shrug – personally, I have always made the time to read verse – but I let it alone. "Quite what would make a man conceal the identity of his own brother's murderers, I cannot imagine," I continued. "And frankly, it's not worth my time to find out. But it is worth my time to seek justice for George's widow and his children, and for his friends – myself included." I leaned forward and banged my fist on the crate to get Ryder's attention. He jumped in his seat and looked at me, fear in his eyes. "Oh, don't you worry, Mr Ryder," I said, "I'm not going to ask you to search for whatever scrap of bravery may be lurking in your soul. All you need to do is tell me how your brother became entangled with the Greenway boys, and I'll do the rest. I gave my word to Mrs Ryder, and that poor woman does not need more disappointment."

At half-past five I stood in the stables, brushing down the horses that had pulled in the *Telegraph*. The rhythmic movement of the brush over the horse's body and the answering shiver of its flanks was familiar and comforting, and as I worked I reflected on what Bill Ryder had eventually confessed. Last September he had been asked to supply fish to the kitchen of St Clement's College – a good piece of work for him, regular and well-paid. Twice a week Ryder would wheel his barrow to the college, loaded with his choicest fish, for the cook to select what he wanted. Once a month Ryder would submit his bill to the kitchen, and on his next visit the cook would pay him what was owing. No arguments about price, no delays in payment – any other man would have been satisfied.

I backed the horse I had been tending into its stable, shut the door, and led its neighbour out. A quick check of its hooves showed that all was well, and I started brushing again, the animal turning its head lazily to follow my movements.

But it seems that Mary Ryder had been right about her husband's brother: he was always looking for a way to make easy money. And when, on his regular visits to the kitchen of St Clement's, he started to hear rumours, he thought to turn them to his advantage. There were whispers among the kitchen staff that the butler was using his position in the college to line his own pockets. I knew from conversations I had overheard in the Sun, and from the evidence of my own eyes as I moved around the town, that university fellows and scholars had little time for the practical details of life. And the residents of a college are a captive population when it comes to food and drink. It was well known that some cunning college staff would charge over the odds for items ordered from the buttery, or ensure that so much food was ordered from suppliers that there was always a plentiful amount of waste that could walk back out of the door.

I assumed that Bill Ryder was going to tell me that he had seen his chance, and had offered to deliver more fish to the kitchen, on the understanding that the proceeds from the sale of any leftovers would be divided between him and the butler. But it seems that Bill's ambitions had outgrown simple larceny, and he had decided to try his hand at blackmail. His plan, he told me with some pride, had been to let the butler know that his dishonesty had been discovered and to propose that a modest, regular payment would keep his secret. And out of filial affection – as he told it – he had offered to cut George in, suggesting that they could both make a tidy little income from it, but George had wanted no part of it.

"But you did tell him everything you had heard?" I had asked. "About St Clement's and the butler?"

Ryder had looked defensive. "I just thought that with all those mouths to feed, he could do with a bit more money coming in."

"But instead, Mr Ryder," I had said, "you made him a target. Anyone involved in the theft from the college would need to silence whoever knew about it. And it seems they may have found your brother before they found you."

"So you think I could be in danger, do you?" he had asked, looking around him as though assassins might be lurking in the eaves.

"Oh, I very much hope so, Mr Ryder," I had answered, and I had meant it.

Just then I heard a rumble of wheels on cobbles and a loud halloo. I had been so busy with my own thoughts that the *Leicester* had arrived and driven into an empty yard. I quickly pushed the horse back into his stable, closed the door, shrugged on my coat and went outside to apologise to the driver.

Chapter Five

BUTLER

In a college, as in a coaching inn, the early mornings are hectic. For that reason, I waited until I had seen the *Telegraph* on its way to London before I splashed my hands and face with water to rinse off the smell of horses and hay and put on my coat. I held open the door for a maid who was staggering to the laundry under a pile of crumpled bed linen and walked into the inn to tell Mr Bird where I was going. But when I reached his room the door was closed and I could hear raised voices. This was nothing new; everyone who worked at the Sun knew that William Bird and his partner John Mills often had disagreements about how the place should be run. For my money, Mr Bird was the more natural innkeeper and had a better business mind, while the shyer Mr Mills would have been better suited to a quieter life – perhaps a country clergyman. Not wishing to interrupt them, I caught the sleeve of the pot boy as he came out of the dining room on his way to the kitchen and told him that if anyone asked I would be back by noon.

It was a bitter morning. The storms of previous days had passed – much to the relief of Mrs Jacobs and her roof – but behind them had come a frigid cold that settled on us. I was thankful for the absence of the knife-like wind for which these parts of the country are known, but the stillness brought something else. Wet fog crept around the streets in the mornings, clearing for a few hours in the middle of the day and then returning at dusk, like a vengeful cat slinking along an alleyway. I turned up the coat of my collar, hunched my shoulders, pushed my hands deep into my pockets, and headed north along Trinity Street. A clutch of scholars hurried past me, separating like a stream going around a rock before closing together again and then stepping wordlessly, one by one, through the small wooden door in the large wooden gate to St John's College. I turned into Bridge Street, crossed over and ducked into the narrow street running down the side of the church. There was a row of tall houses, their upper storeys hanging over me, which gave way to a high wall on my right. Behind this, I knew, were the gardens of St Clement's College. Although calling them gardens was perhaps a little generous; St Clement's was not a wealthy college, and its land was mostly given over to orchard and vegetables rather than to anything decorative.

At a break in the wall there was the entrance to the college: a dark wooden frame topped by a crest which had seen better days. The wooden anchor at its centre was missing a couple of links from its chain, and the generous coating of droppings suggested that birds used its arm as a roost. A carved ribbon beneath the anchor had the college motto picked out on it in faded gold lettering: *Dirige nos ad caelum serenum et mare tranquillum*. When I was a boy my mother – recognising my curiosity – had sent me to be drilled in the basics of Latin by Mr Roberts, the nervous young clergyman at St Nicholas in Bracon Ash. And my months in Cambridge had made me want to learn more, so I quickly took the little vocabulary book from my pocket and jotted down the words to decipher later.

The heavy college door was tightly closed and I had to put my shoulder to it to push it open. I stepped through into the stone-flagged porch and knocked on the small window of the porters' lodge. The shutter on the inside was pulled back and the porter's face appeared. Like me, he was muffled against the cold; wealthier colleges might provide for their porters to have coals all winter long, day and night, but not this one.

"Your business?" he asked, his experienced glance immediately telling him that I was no scholar or fellow. His eyes widened slightly as he took in my face.

"I wish to speak to the butler," I said.

"Mr Perry?" he said. "And what business might you have with Mr Perry? If you're selling, it's the cook you'll need to see." He looked down to check whether I was carrying anything.

I shook my head. "I'm not selling," I said. I had already decided that I would probably have to stretch the truth a little. "I am here in connection with an inquest, and I need to speak to Mr Perry himself. About an allegation." It was a good word – it had weight and authority.

And it interested the porter; his eyebrows shot up and he moved away from the window. I heard the bolt on the door being scraped back and he appeared.

"Follow me," he said. As we walked into the college court, he asked casually, "An allegation against Mr Perry?"

"An allegation," I repeated. Cambridge was a growing town, it was true, but it was still nothing more than a village when it came to gossip. And I knew that if I let anything slip to this man, it would be public news by the time I returned to the Sun.

"The staircase just this side of the dining hall," he said, pointing. "First floor."

I nodded my thanks and walked around the court to the staircase he had indicated. Just inside the entrance was the door to the dining hall; it would be empty at this time of day, and indeed when I stuck my head around the door out of sheer curiosity, the only person within was a man on his hands and knees scrubbing the floor. Women's work in most places, aye, but the colleges thought it wise to employ as few women as possible, to avoid putting temptation into the way of the scholars. At least that was what they told the world; personally, I thought the temptation would be more for the fellows, forbidden to marry and shut up for long years with only cold books for company. Women were employed as bedmakers and laundresses, but all other jobs were given to men. I closed the door quietly and went up the stone staircase to the first floor. Here two doors faced each other; the one directly above the dining hall had "BUTLER" written on it in careful gold script. I knocked.

"Come," a voice said.

I opened the door and stepped into the butler's room. It was not at all what I was expecting, which was a slightly more elegant version of Mr Bird's room at the Sun. No: this was a far grander space. A generous fire burned in a tall stone fireplace which was entirely surrounded by wood panelling. On the pillars of the panelling were carvings that put me in mind of the churches I had seen in Spain, with grapes spilling out of urns, and vines and leaves curling upwards. The panelling continued around the windows, which were tall and fine and looked out over the court I had crossed. Against one wall was an open writing desk, its surface covered with papers, while untidy folders and more papers formed unsteady piles on the floor alongside it. In the centre of the room was a dainty table where three people at most could have dined, and flanking the fireplace were two comfortable winged armchairs. In one of these sat the butler of St Clement's College, Mr Robert Perry. He had a ledger open on his lap; he deliberately put a finger on it to mark his place and then looked up at me.

"And you are?" he said. He had done well to adopt the tone of a Cambridge man but I could hear the country boy behind it – Suffolk, I would guess.

"My name is Gregory Hardiman," I said. "I am here about the death of George Ryder."

"I do not know any George Ryder," he said.

"Perhaps you know his brother, then," I said easily. "William Ryder. Bill to his friends. Sells fish."

"Ah," said Perry, his eyebrows raising a little. "Ryder. Fish. Yes, that is familiar. I am sure I have seen his name in the cook's accounts."

"Could I see those accounts, Mr Perry?" I asked.

The butler's head reared back. "Certainly not, Mr..."

"Hardiman," I repeated.

"Indeed," he said. "Well, surely you don't imagine, Mr Hardiman, that anyone can simply wander in here and demand to see private College documents." He reached over to a small side table and picked up a bookmark which he put into the ledger he was holding before closing it firmly.

"Not anyone, no," I agreed. "But a coroner, perhaps, or the Proctor."

"The Proctor!" he repeated, standing abruptly. Rattled, I would say. "And what interest might the Proctor, or a coroner, have in our ledgers? Are they taking a census of how many herrings we eat?" His eyes narrowed. "And more to the point, Mr Hardiman: why would they send you?"

"I did not say that they had sent me, Mr Perry," I replied.

I could all but see the butler's mind working, as he went back over what had been said. "No more you did, Mr Hardiman," he admitted. He walked over to his desk and added the ledger he was carrying to its weight of papers. He paused for a few seconds and then turned to me with a friendlier look on his face; he had obviously decided that charm might work better than temper. He indicated the armchairs. "Take a seat, Mr Hardiman, and warm yourself. And you can tell me what interest you have in how much fish our cook buys."

I took one of the armchairs and gratefully extended my hands to the fire; East Anglian winters had been hard enough on our farm when I was a lad, but now that my joints were twenty years older the cold seemed to take up residence in them in November and stubbornly refuse to let go until April. The butler sat in the other chair and looked expectantly at me.

"George Ryder drowned in the river, by the Great Bridge, a week ago," I started. "At the inquest, it became clear that it was not an accident – that Mr Ryder was knocked senseless before being thrown into the water. Hit here," I indicated my own forehead, "with a cudgel. A nasty attack. His widow asked me for help, as I had known her husband, and I promised that I would try to find out why anyone would want to harm the cook at a coaching inn. And it seems that the attack on George was meant as a warning to his brother – a warning that went too far."

Perry frowned slightly. "You mean the brother who supplies fish to us here at college?"

I nodded.

"But why would anyone need to warn a man who sells fish?" mused the butler. "A competitor, you think?"

I leaned forward in my chair. "Mr Perry," I said sternly, "do not take me for a fool. You cannot think that I have come here without good reason. I have spoken to William Ryder, and at least he sees the danger he is in." Some of the colour left Perry's face but he said nothing. "I know that you and he have an arrangement. That he supplies fish to St Clement's and inflates the amount on his invoices, and that you and the cook approve these invoices and that you each take your cut from the amount the college pays out to Ryder." The butler took a breath as though to speak, then thought better of it. "What I do not know is whether the Bursar is also involved – I shall have to ask him."

I gripped the arms of the chair as though readying to stand, and the butler's arm shot out to stop me.

"The Bursar knows nothing of this," he said through gritted teeth. "He is," he paused to find the right word, "disinclined to involve himself in the minutiae of college finances."

I raised a disbelieving eyebrow. "But he is the Bursar," I said. "The man charged with overseeing those very finances."

The butler stood and walked over to the window, then turned to face me again. "Mr Hardiman, are you familiar with the way in which a college is organised?"

"I know that there is a master," I said, "and that beneath him there are fellows." He nodded and I continued. "I assume that the fellows teach the undergraduates."

"Some of them, yes," said Perry. "Some of the fellows do teach – we call them tutors. And some of the fellows take on other duties within the college. Our Praelector, for instance, presents our undergraduates for their degrees. That's quite a popular role, as he is paid a nice little stipend – six pounds a year – for very little work."

I held up a hand. "Praelector?" I said. "Can you spell that for me?" I took the vocabulary book out of my pocket and waited.

The butler looked a little surprised but did as he was asked and I carefully wrote down the new word. "From the Latin," he added. "One who reads aloud." I noted that too. Another word like maelstrom, with the letters in that order.

Perry continued. "Our bursar is, as you say, responsible for overseeing the finances of the college. It is a much less popular role: although the stipend is more generous, at twenty pounds a year, the work is much more onerous. The bursar has to look at accounts, check that they balance each year, approve payments, attend meetings, receive begging letters – and on it goes. Not many men put their name forward, and anyone who is willing to take it on might find himself stuck with it for years. The St Clement's bursar, for example, has been in post for, oh, it must be fifteen years now." The butler came and sat down again. He spoke in a lower tone. "And in all those years he has learned nothing about financial matters. He signs whatever is put in front of him – by me, or the cook, or tradesmen from the town."

"And so you and the cook take full advantage of this," I said.

The butler looked affronted. "You would do well to remember your place, Mr Hardiman." He closed his eyes for a moment and then continued in more conciliatory tones. "Forgive me. Despite the grand surroundings," he waved his arm to take in his own room and the college court beyond, "the life of a college butler is not an easy one. I am at the beck and call of the fellows and the undergraduates. I have to provide meals to meet their exacting requirements every single day, and to conjure grand feasts out of a niggardly purse. They dress me as a gentleman," he indicated his fine clothes, "but treat me as a servant. Is it small wonder, then, that I seek to augment my modest salary?"

"So you have been stealing from the college, in agreement with William Ryder?" I said calmly.

"Yes and no," he said. "In the past, when I was junior butler, yes, I did enter into mutually beneficial arrangements with a small number of tradesmen. But that is, as I say, in the past. When I became butler I decided that the risk was not worth it and I called a halt to all of it. I have been butler for three years now, and I've kept my slate clean. If Bill Ryder told you he's paying me, he's lying."

"And is there still a junior butler?" I asked.

"Yes," said Perry. "Philip Lowe. I selected him personally, when I rose to the position of butler. I was appointed by Mr Graves when he was butler, and when he died I took his position and appointed my own junior man."

"My goodness, yes," said Mrs Jacobs as she spooned the stew into my bowl. In all honesty she is but a middling cook and I could eat better in town, but I know she welcomes the company. And this evening she was paying for my company with valuable information, so we were both happy with the deal. She put a much smaller portion into her own bowl, returned the ladle to the pot and then sat opposite me. "You might think that the butler and cook and so on are part of the college staff, but they're not: they run their own businesses. They are attached to a college, you might say, but left pretty much to their own devices." She took a spoonful of stew and then delicately wiped her mouth. "Mr Jacobs, God rest him, had plenty to say about it."

I nodded. "He was a coalman, wasn't he?" I asked.

"A coal merchant," she corrected me. "His firm supplied several of the colleges, but it was all done through the butlers and the cooks. As I understand it, the butler would order coal for the fellows and undergraduates and for the public rooms in the college, and the cook would order for the kitchens. My husband would put in his bills to the butler or the cook, and – I think this is right – they would pass them on to the bursar and he would settle with them out of the college money. And then the butler or the cook would pay my husband."

"So plenty of room for the butler or cook to charge a bit extra for the trouble," I observed.

"Oh yes," she agreed. "That's why being a college butler is such a good job." She leaned forwards and dropped her voice, although with only Mr Carey in the house and him – as she so often reminded me – as deaf as an adder, I wasn't sure who she thought might be listening. "My George said that the butler of St John's earns more than £200 a year – more than the most senior fellow in the place!"

Chapter Six

Master

"You again," observed the porter at St Clement's. This time I had caught him on the way back from the privy, judging by the way he was adjusting himself beneath his coat.

"Me again," I agreed.

"And what's your business this time?" he said, turning the key in the door to his lodge. "Perhaps you want to talk to the Proctor about a murder? Or to the Vice-Chancellor about treason?" He chuckled, delighted at his own wit, as he went into the lodge and closed the door behind him. Just as last time, I had to tap on the small window until he opened the shutter.

"I would like to see Mr Lowe," I said, keeping the irritation out of my voice – I would give him no excuse to deny my request.

"The junior butler will be in the pantry at this time of day," he said. "Stock-taking. Does it at the start of every term. Same door as last time, but go through the dining hall on the ground floor. Go into the kitchen and ask someone to direct you to the pantry." And he closed the shutter.

I did as instructed; a young lad sitting on a stool in the busy kitchen and peeling an enormous pile of potatoes paused long enough to point with his knife at a door standing ajar, while staring open-mouthed at my face. I walked towards the door, ducking to avoid being brained by a tray of loaves carried on the shoulder of another lad, and peered through into a room furnished floor to ceiling with rough wooden shelves.

"Mr Lowe?" I called into the gloom.

"A moment, if you please," came the reply, followed shortly by a tall, spare man of about my own age.

"You are the junior butler?" I asked before I could stop myself.

"Junior in rank, not in years," replied Lowe – it was obviously a query he was used to. He wore dark trousers and a coat of similar dark cloth, and protected both with a long canvas apron, of the sort favoured by butchers. Cradled in the crook of his left arm was an open ledger, while his right hand held a stub of pencil. Unable to shake my hand, he nodded, his eyes sliding to and then quickly away from my scars. "Philip Lowe. And you are Mr Hardiman, I believe." He smiled at my surprise. "Mr Perry said I should expect to see you." He looked down at his ledger, made a final mark in it and slipped the pencil into the pocket on the front of his apron before closing the ledger. "Shall we have our discussion in the dining hall? We shall be undisturbed there."

He led me back through the kitchen, weaving expertly between counters and baskets and people. The dining hall was mercifully quiet after the hubbub of the kitchen and we took two seats facing each other at the end of one of the three long tables leading up to the high table.

"Did Mr Perry tell you why I would be calling to see you?" I asked.

"He said you were interested in the college's dealings with Bill Ryder, the fishmonger," replied Lowe. "That Ryder's brother had died and you were asking questions for the widow." He looked closely at my face – at my scars, I assumed, but I was wrong. "And you think that Mr Perry did not tell you everything." It was a statement, not a question.

"And why would I think that?" I asked. "Is Mr Perry dishonest?"

The junior butler shook his head. "I need this position, Mr Hardiman," he said. "I have responsibilities."

"We all have responsibilities, Mr Lowe," I said. "And one of mine is to make sure that my friend's widow does not spend the rest of her days wondering why her husband was killed. Let me tell you what I know. I know that Bill Ryder and Mr Perry had an arrangement for several years, where each would skim a little off the top when fish was sold to this college. I know that when a man does that once, he usually does it again, and so I suspect that there were other arrangements with other suppliers. I know that Mr Perry told me he stopped it all when he was promoted to butler. And I am wondering whether to believe him." Lowe's eyes widened but he said nothing. I continued. "I also know that Ryder's brother did not just die – he was killed. Not a deliberate killing, maybe, but a vicious attack – those responsible had no care for his life. They wanted it to serve as a warning to Ryder, and perhaps as a warning to others involved with him." I leaned forward and looked intently at the man opposite me. "Perhaps as a warning to you." I sat back again. "As a man with responsibilities, Mr Lowe, you might be wise to think about that."

I could see from the expression on his face that he was doing exactly that. To give him time to come to a decision, I let my gaze wander around the dining hall, from the severe portraits on the wall – well-fed, satisfied-looking college dignitaries to a man – to the delicate wood carving around the ceiling, picked out in red and gold paint that was now flaking. The door to the kitchen opened and a boy of no more than eight or nine tottered in almost hidden beneath a large stack of plates; he deposited them with a clatter on the table furthest from us and breathed a sigh of relief. Then he caught sight of us and paused for a moment to gawp at me before scurrying back into the kitchen.

"Tell me, Mr Hardiman," said Lowe at last. "Do you consider yourself a good man?"

I was surprised, but I answered anyway. "I do my best," I said. "I have done things that I did not imagine doing, and some of them I regret. But I always did them for reasons that seemed good to me at the time." The junior butler listened carefully. "I never set out to do wrong," I concluded.

Lowe nodded. "My father was a man of the church," he said, "and his teachings are not easily forgotten. No more they should be." He took a breath. "My sin is one of omission rather than commission. Isn't that what they say?" I shrugged, and he continued. "When Mr Perry was junior butler and I was just a kitchen hand, I knew what he was doing. I was in the larder one day, cleaning the shelves, when I overheard him talking to Ryder. I confronted Mr Perry, saying that I would go to the Bursar, and he made me an offer: he said that when he was made butler he would appoint me his junior, and that one day I would be butler myself."

"And able to make your own deals with tradesmen," I observed.

Lowe shook his head. "I am not interested in that sort of thing myself. An honest day's work for an honest wage. And I need that wage – there are others who rely on me." He looked shamefaced. "So I convinced myself that saying nothing about Mr Perry and his arrangements was not the same as doing it myself."

"That's a subtlety that might be lost on the Greenway brothers," I said grimly. "The man they killed simply had the bad luck to be Bill Ryder's brother. If they fear an end to whatever arrangement they have with Mr Perry, who knows how they might choose to warn him."

The junior butler went pale. "Do you mean that I am in danger?" he asked.

"As I said," I replied, "the Greenway brothers are careless with people. My advice to you, Mr Lowe, would be to put yourself firmly on the side of the angels, and tell me everything you know so that I can work quickly to see that they are stopped."

I was walking back towards Bridge Street when I heard footsteps hurrying behind me. My mind on the Greenway brothers, I clenched my fists and stepped closer to the wall: if I was to be attacked, I'd be ready for it, protecting one flank.

"Mr Hardiman," called my pursuer. It was the porter from St Clement's.

I released my fists and turned to face him.

"It's the Master, sir," he said, more civil than I had heard him on either of my visits. "He's asked to see you." He saw me hesitate. "Now, if you can, sir."

"Very well," I agreed, and followed him back the way I had come.

We walked across the court to the furthest corner and through the stone archway. Winding up ahead of us was a stone staircase that was the twin of the one I had used to reach the butler's room. A heavy arched door was to our left and the porter nodded his head towards it.

"Chapel," he said. "Upstairs." And he went up the staircase. On the first floor were two more sturdy doors. The one leading to the room above the chapel had no sign on it. Again the porter nodded his head at it. "The Master's teaching room," he explained. The other door bore a shining brass plaque proclaiming that it was the Master's Lodge. The porter knocked smartly on it, and it was opened promptly by a footman. "Mr Hardiman for the Master," said the porter and stepped to one side, inclining his head at me before returning down the staircase.

The footman opened the door wider and indicated that I should take one of the three chairs in the vestibule while he went to announce me. Like the butler's room, this was panelled with wood, but of a plainer design. I barely had time to sit down before the footman returned and asked me to follow him. I walked through into one of the most beautiful rooms I have ever seen.

Years ago Lucia had taken me into a church in Montehermoso dedicated to Our Lady. It wasn't the grandest church but you could tell that it had been built by men who loved their work. Each detail of the vaulted ceiling and the wooden altarpiece was created with pride and adoration, and the devotion of those men seemed to warm and soften the very air in the church. Lucia and I had sat in silence, our shoulders touching, gazing at the humble beauty around us. And afterwards we had laughed that surely our love had been blessed by those craftsmen of so long ago.

And this room had something of that aura. As in the butler's room, there were wooden panels and columns, with beautiful carving. But here, the addition of tall bookcases stretching almost to the ceiling and filled with books that had obviously been read rather than simply stored gave the space a feeling of ancient learning, of hours spent in contemplation and study. My fingers itched to explore those volumes and instinctively I stretched out my hand.

"You are a reader, Mr Hardiman?" asked the man coming towards me.

"I am, sir, yes, when I have the time and the money," I replied. "Gregory Hardiman."

"Francis Vaughan, Master of St Clement's," he offered in return. We shook hands. He was about my own height, perhaps twenty years my senior, and I felt in his grip and saw in his shape the shadow of a once strong and fit man. "Come: let us sit by the fire and warm ourselves. The kitchen has sent up hot coffee and fruit buns."

We settled ourselves into the worn but comfortable armchairs drawn close to the fireplace. Between them was a low table holding a coffee pot and a plate of buns, and the Master busied himself pouring drinks and handing refreshments to me.

"This is good," I said, indicating the bun.

"We are lucky at St Clement's," said Vaughan. "We have two very competent cooks: one can work wonders with any meat or fish you care to give him, and the other has a light hand with sweet things like pastries and puddings. I'm of the view that the better we can feed the men here in college, the less temptation there is for them to visit the taverns and hotels in town."

"I believe you have a good wine cellar too," I said. "With the same aim, I suppose."

Vaughan smiled. "You have seen through me, Mr Hardiman. There are other pleasures a man will seek in town, but food and drink we can provide." I raised an eyebrow. "Have I shocked you, Mr Hardiman, with my worldliness?" he asked.

"Perhaps a little," I admitted. I put my cup down on the low table. "If I am honest, Mr Vaughan, I know nothing about you. I did not know I would be meeting you, otherwise I would have asked about you. I like to be prepared."

"Francis Richard Vaughan," he said promptly, "aged fifty-four. Widowed – no children living. Parents both deceased, two younger sisters living at the family home in Ipswich. Shall I continue?" I nodded, smiling. "By trade a mathematician, with a special interest in algebra. Other interests include reading," he indicated the bookcases, "card games, Lieder (listening, not performing), and horse racing. I will admit to being something of a gambler, Mr Hardiman – it's only arithmetic, after all." He leaned forward and topped up my coffee. "Is that enough?" he asked.

"Coffee, or information?" I asked in turn.

He laughed. "Information."

"It is, sir, yes," I said, smiling. "Although I am curious to know how long you have been here, at St Clement's."

"I graduated from St Clement's in, let me think, 1792. I was elected a fellow six years later, and then Master in 1813. My dear Louisa was with me then, and our two little girls – these rooms were full of laughter and noise. Some of the fellows quite disapproved." He smiled at the memory and then saddened. "We lost Mary to the fever in 1815, and Lucy the following year to chincough. Louisa was brought low by grief, and when she sickened herself she had not the heart to fight back. By the end of 1817 I was rattling around in here on my own, with only my dry old books for company." He smiled again, but it was a pale smile. "Do you have family in Cambridge, Mr Hardiman?" he asked.

I shook my head. "I am a Norfolk boy," I said. "From a village near Norwich."

"And now making a name for yourself in Cambridge," he said, "if our coroner entrusts you with his enquiries."

I held up a hand. "I am not here on the instruction of Mr Ingle. I hope you have not been given a false impression of my authority."

"And what then is your authority, Mr Hardiman?" asked the Master.

"I am simply helping a widow who deserves to know exactly why her husband died – why he was killed," I said. "He was attacked and died of his injuries, and I believe that it was meant as a warning for his brother. And his brother supplies St Clement's – and other colleges – with fish."

"A fishmonger?" asked Vaughan.

"Yes," I said. "Bill Ryder. A rogue, by all accounts, in that he is known to... add a little something for himself to the bills he submits to butlers. Some butlers are genuinely unaware and pay whatever they are asked for, but others – the more worldly ones, perhaps – know what he is about and offer to turn a blind eye in exchange for their own cut."

The Master looked shocked. "And you think that a butler became greedy, demanded more, and when this Mr Ryder refused, they killed his brother as a warning to him?" He shook his head. "Mr Hardiman, it sounds very far-fetched to me."

"No, no," I said. "It's certainly one possibility, but I think it unlikely that a college butler would let things go so far. Other, more desperate men might however." I leaned forward in my seat. "Mr Vaughan, there is a local family – a roguish gang called the Greenway brothers. I think they have seen the potential in these arrangements between Ryder and the colleges. I think they approach those involved and threaten them with exposure or worse, and before you know where you are, the Greenways are bleeding your college dry."

"A graphic description, Mr Hardiman," said the Master. "You have spoken to Mr Perry and to Mr Lowe – do you think they are paying money to these Greenway brothers?"

"Mr Perry was adamant that he is no longer padding the invoices," I replied. "And Mr Lowe denied ever having done so."

"I asked what you think, Mr Hardiman," said Vaughan, "not what they said." A sharp brain indeed.

"I will be as straight with you as you are with me, Mr Vaughan," I said. "I am more inclined to believe Mr Lowe than Mr Perry." The Master nodded and I continued. "And I am also inclined to think that the Greenway brothers will continue until they are stopped."

"You think they will continue stealing?" he asked.

"I think they will continue hurting people," I clarified.

"In that case, Mr Hardiman, our way forward is clear," said Vaughan. "You may not have Mr Ingle's authority but you now have mine. If you are willing, I would like you to continue with your enquiries, so that we may put Mrs Ryder's mind at rest. We should also do our best to bring the Greenway brothers to justice. And if you can achieve this with discretion, so that the name of St Clement's is not dragged through the mire, I should be extremely grateful. We are a small college with few wealthy connections and we cannot afford to lose even a single matriculation fee. As it is, we have only two men to take to the Senate House tomorrow." I must have looked puzzled. "For their matriculation ceremony – when they sign the Registrary's book and are officially admitted to the University. Only two. And one of them a sizar." He shook his head sadly.

Chapter Seven

Apothecary

I shivered as I stepped out through the college gate and was grateful for the warm pockets of my coat. With my right hand I felt the familiar shape of the small brown bottle, with its rounded corners and its cork stopper, fitting comfortingly into my palm. I shook it gently. Only a few left. I turned into Bridge Street and almost immediately ducked into the shadowed overhang of St Sepulchre's Passage. The door to Mr Relhan's shop was shut tight against the cold, but inside I could see the apothecary at his counter, bent over his pestle and mortar. I went in.

Mr Relhan looked up. "Mr Hardiman," he said and smiled in welcome. By inclination Mr Relhan was an artist, and he spent his free time sketching and painting the world around him, whether that was natural or created by man. I once saw him perched on a folding stool near the castle, and he showed me a very accomplished and accurate picture of the gatehouse and the hill behind it. But it is difficult to make a living from sketches, and as a lad he had been apprenticed to an apothecary. He now ran his own shop, living above it with his younger brother and his sister-in-law.

"Mr Relhan," I said, closing the door behind me. I could buy my opium from many shops in Cambridge, of course, but I liked the cleanliness of Mr Relhan's establishment, and I knew the pride he took in his preparations. Having seen the rubbish sold in other places – and having felt the ill effects on one or two occasions – I preferred to pay a little more and deal with a man who understood what he was about. I looked up at the shelves filling the wall behind the counter, each large jar carrying a neat label in the apothecary's careful script – as you might imagine for an artist, he had a beautiful hand.

Relhan put the pestle and mortar to one side. I took the brown bottle from my pocket and gave it to him. He removed the stopper and tipped the remaining tablets onto a dark cloth. "Six," he said, glancing up at me, and I nodded. He pushed them carefully to one edge of the cloth. "And you would like fifty-six more? To last another month?"

"If you please," I confirmed.

He reached behind him and took down one of the smaller jars. He lifted off the lid and poured out a cascade of tablets onto the cloth. With the tip of his finger he rapidly counted the tablets, moving them to one side as he went. He looked up at me. "Nearly," he said with glee, and extracted one final tablet from the jar before replacing the lid and returning the jar to the shelf. He put a small funnel into the neck of my bottle, gathered up the cloth and poured in all the tablets. He pushed in the stopper and handed the bottle back to me. I tucked it away into one coat pocket and from the other I took the two shillings I owed him.

"And the reduced dose...?" he asked as he put the coins into a drawer. "You find it sufficient?"

"Most of the time," I replied.

Relhan looked at me with curiosity. "But there are times when it is not?" he asked.

"It is harder in winter," I admitted. "In the lighter months, I can go for a long walk. I can, I don't know, hear the birds and smell the flowers. They tempt me to go outside, to make myself move." I shrugged. "But in the winter – the darkness, the solitude."

"But did you not tell me that a larger dose makes you even more lethargic?" asked the apothecary. He reached under the counter and brought out a notebook. He paged through it. "Yes: here it is. Lethargy and lack of interest in the world. That was on the larger dose – November last year."

I should explain, I suppose. When I first went to Relhan's shop on my arrival in Cambridge and explained my needs, and we found that we liked each other, he asked whether he could keep a note of my doses and the effects, for his own understanding of the drug. Most of his customers preferred laudanum and other opium tinctures, and he was keen to learn more about the pure form. I agreed: I admired his professional curiosity.

"And that is true," I agreed. "But sometimes lethargy is what I need. Sometimes," I closed my eyes for a moment, "sometimes the energy of the world is too much."

The apothecary looked at me, gave a tight nod and made a note in his book.

Chapter Eight

BOUNCERS

You will forgive me for mentioning again the mists that torment us in Cambridge, and how they sink and cling like a damp and unwelcome blanket. It was into one such bone-chilling murk that I turned out after my Sunday supper. It was a quiet day at the Sun – as at all inns in town – but I had to be there to meet the *Safety* and the *Tally Ho*. Run by competing companies, they both provided a service for those wishing to travel from the capital and – if the conditions were favourable, which they rarely were in winter – would arrive in Cambridge a half-hour apart. The first was due at half-past eight, but I liked to be in the stables an hour before that to prepare the stalls. I called my farewell to Mrs Jacobs, tucked up by her fireside with her basket of needlework, and stepped out into Jesus Lane just as the church called seven with muffled chimes. As my lodgings were on the edge of fields the fog was at its thickest. But I had walked this route many times and judged that very few horses would be out at this hour and so I turned my step confidently towards town.

I had gone only a few yards when I heard footsteps approaching behind me and ahead of me at the same time. I assumed it was the fog playing tricks with the sound until a shove to my back almost sent me sprawling. As I struggled to regain my balance, my arms were roughly grabbed and I was propelled into a small alleyway.

"I have very little money on me," I gasped, "but you are welcome to it."

"We're not interested in your fadges," growled a rough voice. "We just want a quiet word with you, Mr Hardiman."

I looked around me, my eyes adjusting to the gloom, and made a show of straightening my coat and dusting down my sleeves. There were two men squeezed into the alley with me. Both were taller than me, bulky, and obviously brothers.

"You could have come to the Sun for that, Mr Greenway," I said. "You know where it is."

"So there's no need for any introductions," said the slightly shorter of the two. And he was right: I was certain he was Jem Greenway. "If you know who we are, you'll know what we're here to say."

"Stop asking questions and let sleeping dogs lie?" I asked.

The taller man guffawed until a glance from his brother silenced him.

"Precisely," said Jem. He moved even closer to me and I could smell the ale on his breath. "I hear you're a clever man, Mr Hardiman. Know poetry and all sorts. And I can tell from this," he raised a hand and indicated my face, "that you've seen some action. You'll remember the pain of that." He waited for a response but I wasn't going to play his game. He continued. "If you're tempted to stick your nose in my business again, just remember that pain."

"Did you speak this warmly to George Ryder before you murdered him?" I asked.

The silent brother moved towards me but Jem held up a hand to halt him.

"As the coroner said," said Jem in a low tone, "no-one knows what happened to George Ryder. So you need to watch yourself if you're going to accuse people of murder." He sniffed. "Things got a bit out of hand with Mr Ryder. We never meant him to go into the water. But he struggled, and it was slippery."

"I'm sure his widow will be comforted to know that you only meant to hurt her perfectly blameless husband, not to kill him," I said. I may have gone too far. For a big man the silent brother moved surprisingly swiftly, and I didn't even see his arm lift. But I certainly felt the hard slap to the back of my head.

"You need to keep a civil tongue in your head, Mr Hardiman," said Jem. "Every man – even an ugly joskin like you – has things he'd hate to lose. There's Mrs Jacobs, for instance. And those stables you work in – be a great shame if they caught alight, wouldn't it. Terrified of fire, horses are." He leaned forward again. "I'm not in the habit of repeating myself, so let's agree that you've heard me loud and clear."

And he and his brother melted away into the fog.

Perhaps a more sensible man would have heeded their warning. But I had made a promise, however rashly, and I was not one to break a promise. And if Boney and his lancers had failed to finish me, I certainly wasn't going to surrender to bouncers like the Greenways.

Chapter Nine

LOSSES

The note was written in a beautiful, educated hand. "Mr Hardiman," it said, "some further matters have come to my attention. Would you be so kind as to attend the Lodge this morning at 11 o'clock. I have consulted the coach timetable and believe that you will be free at that time. I await your response. With sincere good wishes, Francis Vaughan."

I reached into my pocket and found a couple of coins which I gave to the lad who had delivered the message. "Return to whoever sent you from St Clement's," I said, "and tell them that the answer is yes." The lad nodded and touched his forelock, trying not to look too hungrily at the hunk of fresh bread in my other hand; he had found me taking my morning break in the stables. "Here," I said, handing it to him.

"All of it?" he asked, astonished.

"You're growing upwards, I'm growing outwards," I explained. "Off with you."

He took a huge bite and nodded gratefully at me, his cheek bulging.

Francis Vaughan, I suppose from being a mathematician, was a man of precision. The nearby church was tolling the hour as his footman opened the door and invited me to enter. Waiting in the book-lined room were three people: the Master, the junior butler Philip Lowe, and one of the most elderly men I had ever seen. There was barely anything to him, so thin was he; he was almost bald, with only a few feathery strands of grey hair above his ears, and he stood stooped over a walking stick. Nevertheless, when he looked up at me I could see both intelligence and humour in his watery eyes.

The Master walked over to welcome me. "Thank you for agreeing to visit me again so soon, Mr Hardiman," he said warmly. "You have met our junior butler." Lowe and I shook hands. "And this," the Master shepherded me towards the old man, "this is Professor Samuel Sandys, lecturer in theology." I bent down a little to shake the frail hand of Professor Sandys. The old man looked up at my face and smiled gently. "And more pertinent to our discussion today," continued the Master, "Professor Sandys is in charge of our college library. Come now, gentlemen, let us take a seat – Mr Hardiman has important duties to attend to after our meeting, even if the rest of us will simply go back to wearing out our eyes on dusty books." He smiled at me. "Isn't that what the townsfolk say of us?"

I waited until Professor Sandys had settled himself into a chair that Lowe had carefully guided him to and then took my own seat. "Something of that sort, yes," I agreed. I took my black notebook and pencil from my coat pocket. "With your permission?" I asked, and the Master nodded.

As he had done on my previous visit, Vaughan made sure that his guests were provided with refreshments – for my part, I accepted a cup of coffee and another of those excellent buns. He then started to speak.

"When we last met, Mr Hardiman," he said, "you kindly agreed to look into the matter of Mr Ryder and his dealings with St Clements, with an eye to discovering whether his, shall we say, methods had been adopted by other tradesmen." I nodded. "I am not sure whether your enquiries have yet yielded any fruit, but in the meantime we here at St Clement's have made some disturbing discoveries of our own. Mr Lowe, shall we start with you?"

"Thank you, Master," said the junior butler. He reached down and picked up the ledger that he had leaned against the leg of his chair. He opened it to a page marked with a slip of paper and read it for a moment before starting to speak. "As you all know, one of my main duties is to check that the contents of the larder match the records – that is, that we receive the quantity we pay the suppliers for, and then that we use the quantity accounted for by the cook and the butler, which in turn is paid for by the fellows and scholars." He looked at me and I nodded to show that I had understood. He continued. "Given the recent revelations about Mr Ryder, the Master asked me to go back over the ledger for the past year and make more careful checks, and I am partway through this work. But," and here he reached down for a second, smaller ledger, "it occurred to me that the most valuable purchases that the college makes in terms of comestibles is not food, but drink – port, sherry, hock and the like. And so I decided to check the wine ledger first. And I found it very worrying." He opened the wine ledger.

"Forgive me for interrupting," I said, "but isn't the keeping of an accurate wine ledger already your responsibility, Mr Lowe?"

The Master shook his head. "The wine ledger is the responsibility of the butler," he clarified. "Mr Perry, not Mr Lowe. I understand that Mr Lowe has borrowed the ledger for our purposes, and undertakes to replace it before its absence is noted."

The junior butler flushed a little and nodded.

"To my mind," I suggested, "the wine ledger is actually the property of the college. And as such, it is up to the Master to allow anyone he chooses to examine it."

"Quite so," agreed the Master, smiling encouragingly at the junior butler. "Please continue, Mr Lowe."

"Thank you, sir," said Lowe. He looked down at the wine ledger. "Well, it's a little complicated, gentlemen, but I will give some examples. I see here that on the 9th of March last year the college placed an order for a hogshead of sherry with Chalié Richards of Pall Mall in London. It was delivered as twenty-five and a half dozen bottles, at a total cost of just over fifty-six pounds for the sherry, the bottling and the carriage. The bottles were sold to various fellows – most taking three dozen bottles each – with the college buying five dozen bottles for its own use. That should last half a year, perhaps longer. And yet," Lowe turned to another marked page, "a mere three months later, we see a similar order being placed – but this time with Robert Scaplehorn here in Cambridge."

"On Trinity Street, yes," I said, looking up from my notebook in which I had been writing quickly. "Perhaps whoever placed the second order thought the London wine merchant might think it odd to receive a second order so soon after the first, and might contact the Master to check it."

"That was exactly my thought, Mr Hardiman," said the junior butler.

"Are there other similar instances?" I asked. "Repeated orders?"

"Yes," replied Lowe. "There is a doubling up of orders for port, and for sparkling Moselle. And they both follow the same pattern: one order with one merchant, and a second identical order with a different merchant."

"So if the college is buying much more wine than it needs," I asked, although I feared I already knew the answer, "does that mean that your cellars are full to bursting with bottles?"

"Hah!" said Professor Sandys, with a wheezy laugh.

Lowe shook his head. "I have done a very careful count, and we have almost exactly the stock I would expect if we had placed only the standard orders – not the extra ones."

"In other words," I said, looking at the Master for confirmation, "it seems that someone is ordering wine, paying for it from college funds, and then removing it from the cellar. And presumably then selling it on for their own personal profit."

"That seems the most likely explanation," agreed Vaughan. "And it is worrying and distasteful and disloyal. But food and wine can be replaced. What concerns me even more is what Professor Sandys has discovered. Professor Sandys, if you would."

I held up a hand. "A question first, if I may," I said. The Master nodded. "Given that we are discussing college finances," I said carefully, "shouldn't the Bursar be here? As I understand it, a bursar is responsible for overseeing college finances." I looked at the three men questioningly.

The Master cleared his throat. "That is certainly the situation in theory, Mr Hardiman," he said. "But our situation here at St Clement's is a little, shall we say, awkward."

"Hah!" interjected Sandys again, with less humour this time.

Vaughan continued. "Our Bursar is Mr John Galpin. He is the grandson of William Galpin, one of the college's most generous benefactors, and as such his position is all but unassailable. He became our Bursar in 1804 and looks minded to stay in post until, well, who knows."

"So your Bursar holds his position thanks to family connections, and has done so for more than twenty years?" I asked.

"Just so," said the Master. "But I want to make it clear that the college is not negligent in its duties: Mr Galpin is by no means incompetent. He is simply... uninterested. Or rather, his interests lie elsewhere. Mr Galpin is a lecturer in chemistry – his area of research and his greatest interest is gases."

"And the Philosophical Society," added the junior butler.

"Indeed, Mr Lowe," said the Master. "The Philosophical Society on Sidney Street. When Mr Galpin is not teaching or conducting his experiments, that is most likely where you will find him."

"Thank you," I said, making a note of it. "And I apologise for interrupting: Professor Sandys was about to speak."

The old man inclined his head. "Thank you, Mr Hardiman," he said. His voice was clearer than I had expected, and rather warm and gentle, with a long-forgotten Scottish burr to it. "As the Master has explained, I act as librarian for the college. We have a working library of the usual volumes, which I augment quarterly. A regular payment of eight pounds and three shillings is made to me to enable me to purchase what is needed from Nicholson's in town." He looked at me and I nodded. "We also have a more eclectic collection of items that we have acquired over the years, mostly through bequests from the libraries of alumni."

I feared what was coming next. "Are these items valuable?" I asked.

"Priceless, some of them," replied the Master.

"In terms of scholarship," continued Sandys, "they are all valuable, but yes, some are of great financial worth as well. And three of them are missing." He sighed and shook his head. "I blame myself for not mentioning it sooner. I first noticed that they were not on their shelves at the end of Michaelmas term. That is to say, in the middle of December. But fellows sometimes borrow books from the library without telling me, and I wanted to be sure that none of them had the missing volumes before I went any further."

"And now you are sure?" I asked.

"I have spoken to every fellow and every scholar," confirmed Sandys, "and the volumes are no longer in college."

"Might someone be lying to you?" I asked.

"Extremely unlikely," replied the Master. "Professor Sandys is much loved in the college, and anyway, there is no penalty for taking a volume from the collection as long as it is returned."

"Can you tell me the volumes that are missing?" I asked the librarian.

He reached into the pocket of his black coat – a voluminous garment that even from a distance I could see was much mended. "Here," he said, holding out a piece of paper, "I have written them down for you."

I stood and took the paper from him and placed it carefully in my notebook.

"It is very kind of you to help us, Mr Hardiman," said the Master. "If any of us," he indicated his two companions and then himself, "were to start asking questions, word would quickly spread that something is rotten in St Clement's. But you..." He left the sentence unfinished and simply smiled.

"I am happy to do what I can," I said, "although that may be limited to asking questions – I am no magistrate."

"Indeed," said the Master. "Professor Sandys, Mr Lowe, I am sure you have other duties to attend to." The two men rose to their feet, shook my hand and left the room, the younger taking care to hold the door for the elder. Once we could hear them making their way slowly down the stairs, Vaughan started to speak again. "I did not want to mention this in front of others, so as not to cause alarm or prompt speculation, but I have noticed that other items are missing. Other valuable items."

I opened my notebook again and looked encouragingly at the Master.

"Three in particular grieve me," he said sadly. "All works of art are unique, of course, but these, well, they matter deeply to us as a college. The first is a painting, about this size." He held out his hands shoulder-width apart and then indicated a slightly smaller height. "Very old – fifteenth century. Oil on an oak panel, showing Saint Clement. The college records suggest that it is one panel of a triptych," he looked questioningly at me and I nodded, "taken from a church on the Continent – perhaps in Bruges, or Antwerp. It is not an accomplished piece, and the artist is unknown, but there are not many images of Saint Clement and we treasure – we treasured – it."

"And where was this painting hanging in the college?" I asked.

The Master looked embarrassed. "It was not in the college," he explained. "It had been in the chapel, and when I noticed it missing, I assumed it had been sent for cleaning. The candles, you know."

"When was this?" I asked. "When did you notice that it had gone?"

"About a year ago," said Vaughan.

I raised an eyebrow. "A year ago?" I repeated.

He nodded. "To my regret, I forgot about it – when something is no longer on view, there is nothing there to remind you. It is remiss of me."

I made a note. "And the second piece? I asked.

"My favourite of the three," said the Master, "and again, I blame myself for not noticing sooner that it was missing. It stood on a small plinth in the entrance to the chapel, and you know how it is with familiar objects – you simply stop seeing them." He smiled sadly. "It is a small brass gilt statue of an angel, genuflecting. Like this."

He stood and then dropped to one knee, his arms held out in front of him as though offering a long item – a sword, perhaps – to someone.

"What is in the angel's hands?" I asked.

The Master got to his feet and dusted off the knee that had been on the floor. "Nothing," he replied, "but there must once have been something, as the hands look strangely empty. But the statue is from the fifteenth century, like the painting, and who knows what it has seen in those centuries. Its wings are missing too – you can see the little slots on the back where they would have fitted."

"And you said it was small?" I asked, making more notes.

The Master sat down. "Barely six inches tall," he said. "Very easy to spirit away in a pocket or under a coat."

"Is the third piece religious as well?" I asked.

The Master shook his head. "Almost the opposite, in fact. But this is the one that would cause the college the most embarrassment were the loss to be made public."

"How so?" I asked.

"It is a painting of Anne Ferneley, bequeathed to us by an alumnus," he explained. "She was the wife of Sir Thomas Gresham, financier to King Edward VI and Queen Elizabeth and founder of the Royal Exchange. He was educated at Gonville and Caius, and they have his portrait. If Mr Davy were to hear that we have lost the companion portrait of the wife..."

"Is Mr Davy the Master of Gonville and Caius?" I asked.

Vaughan nodded. "A fine fellow in the ordinary run of things," he said, "but some years ago his college suggested that the two portraits should be reunited, and we refused. Now, of course, I wish that we had not."

"Tell me about the painting," I said.

"Oil on a wooden panel," he said, "about the dimensions of a family Bible. Sixteenth century – Sir Thomas and Anne Ferneley married in about 1545 and my guess would be that the portraits were commissioned then. As for our painting, it's a rather drab, dreary affair – it has a dark background and the sitter is a plain woman in plain dress. Although some of the detail may have been lost over the centuries, and we did not display it to advantage. It was in the dining hall, tucked into a dark corner so as not to offend our more traditional members who prefer not to see women as they dine." He smiled impishly. "Personally, I think women can only improve the scenery, but there you go."

I smiled in agreement. "So it seems," I said, glancing down at my notebook before closing it, "that various valuable items have gone missing from St Clements: wine, books and works of art. The thefts have taken place in the past year," I looked at the Master and he nodded, "and you would like to locate and recover the items without making the matter public." He nodded again, more vigorously.

"You will think me vain, Mr Hardiman," he said, "wanting to hide our carelessness. And I will admit that there is something of that in it. But I suspect that we are dealing with people who will take cover and perhaps melt away altogether if they think that we have discovered the losses. While they feel unobserved, perhaps they will also grow careless. If you could make quiet enquiries, Mr Hardiman, we would be most grateful."

And so it was that I found myself trying to discover the truth not only for a widow but also for an entire college.

CHAPTER TEN

BOOKSELLER

I love the smell of books. Perhaps it is the paper, perhaps it is the ink – but most likely it is the promise of knowledge and adventure. There were no books in my childhood home, but Major Howard had travelled with a small chest of them – a campaign bookcase, I believe it was called. It was made of glorious rich red wood, although rather less glorious by the time we had returned it to Cambridge, and the two halves were hinged to close together for protection and transport. Inside was a small library of fifty-one volumes – I knew the number exactly, for I spent many hours with them. There were a few boyhood treasures such as *The History of Sandford and Merton* and *Keeper's Travels in Search of his Master*. And these stood alongside more mature classics including Scott's *Rob Roy* and the Lambs' *Tales from Shakespeare*. It was in this little library that I had first discovered the volume of poetry by Wordsworth and Coleridge that so captured my heart; it was that self-same volume that Major Howard had pressed into my hand shortly before he died. "To my dear friend Gregory," he had written in it, in the shaky scrawl that was all he could manage in his final days. It was, to me, priceless.

The smell of books greeted me as I pushed open the door of Nicholson's. It was a Cambridge landmark, this elegant property at the corner of Trinity Street and Great St Mary's Street, and although the business had been owned for over a year by Mr Stevenson, it was still known by everyone as Nicholson's. Three generations of Nicholson men had built up the most extensive and respected circulating library in town; as the notice on the wall informed everyone, for seven shillings and sixpence a quarter a subscriber could borrow up to fifteen books at a time, changing them as frequently as he wished. To cater for the intellectual demand in Cambridge, the library held up to five hundred copies of some popular titles, with an emphasis on classical and mathematical books. But other titles were also available for "instruction and amusement", as the notice had it, covering seemingly every interest from divinity to biography and from voyages to romances. I was not often flush in the pocket, saving my money to send to Spain, but perhaps twice a year I would call in at Nicholson's to select a volume to add to my modest shelf of books. And the man who always shared his time and his recommendations with me was Geoffrey Giles.

Over the months I had learned that Mr Giles had worked for the business for nearly four decades, after being taken on at the age of fifteen by the first Mr Nicholson. Maps, as the first Mr Nicholson was called by everyone, had employed the lad as an act of charity, but his kindness was repaid many times over. Geoffrey Giles had been one of the brightest scholars at the Free Grammar School, destined for a fellowship at Gonville and Caius, but a series of family tragedies meant that he had to bring in a wage instead. A schoolmaster mentioned it to Maps, and he – only too delighted to find a young man already fluent in Latin and Greek – gave the young Geoffrey a job. And to my eye, no fellowship could have suited Mr Giles better than working in Nicholson's. His own thirst for knowledge was matched by his pleasure in helping others to find knowledge themselves. Early on in our acquaintance he had suggested that I keep a list of new words as I learnt them, and had even given me my first little red notebook for that purpose. I was now on my third.

Geoffrey Giles was standing on a small stepladder, his back to the door, replacing volumes on a shelf. He turned as he heard the door open, put the remaining books on the top step of the ladder, and descended to greet me.

"Mr Hardiman," he said. "Is it time for an addition to your library? I may have something." He bent down and reached under the counter, straightening up to hand me a little volume. "An ugly title, to be sure," he said, shrugging, "but the verse itself is pretty."

I looked at the book: *The Improvisatrice; and Other Poems* read the title page, by LEL.

"A lady poetess," said Giles. "Six editions last year," he added approvingly.

I was tempted, but I handed the book back to him. "Another day, perhaps," I said. "What I need today, Mr Giles, is your help. Your expert help as a librarian and a bookseller."

"In that case," he said, "you had better come through." He beckoned me to follow him into the back of the shop, calling quietly to another man putting books away on another shelf. "Mr Robinson, I am dealing with an enquiry. Fetch me if I am needed."

We went through a heavy curtain concealing a door at the rear of the shop, and through that door into a small and chaotic parlour. As might be expected, every surface and much of the floor was covered in haphazard piles of books.

Giles caught me looking at them. "Well-loved volumes that we cannot bear to discard," he said, smiling apologetically. "A book can withstand only so many loans, you know, and then it starts to fall apart. Some we mend as best we can and give away to sizars and schools, but others are not worth the effort or are not suitable – and those come here for their retirement."

"Are you not tempted to take them home?" I asked, sitting in the rather sagging armchair that the bookseller indicated.

"My father," said Giles, busying himself with putting a battered kettle on the tiny pot-bellied stove in the corner of the parlour, "is a man of great patience and forbearance, but even he has reached the limits of his tolerance for books at home. He worries that they attract vermin, looking for paper for their nests." He turned and smiled at me. "I smuggle in a volume now and again, but it's a tricky business." He put his hand to the side of the kettle. "Tea, Mr Hardiman? It's from Barker's – a good blend."

"Yes, please," I said. "Most welcome on this chilly morning."

Once we were both settled with our warm drinks, Giles looked at me expectantly. I took my notebook from the pocket of my coat and pulled out the slip of paper that Professor Sandys had given me.

"Three books have disappeared from a college library," I began. "I am told that they are valuable – very rare. If that is the case, they will not be of any use to your normal rogue: they will have been stolen to order, or at least sold to a specialist."

"I certainly hope so," said Giles. "The thought of rare books falling into amateur hands and being discarded, or destroyed..." He shook his head. "May I see the list?" I handed it to him. "My goodness," he said after reading it. "This is a most grievous loss for the college."

"The books are valuable, then?" I asked.

"Irreplaceable," he said, shaking his head sadly. "The eleventh century illuminated psalter from Byzantium – they were mostly created for holy houses, but what with the Crusades and the dissolution of the monasteries, the surviving ones ended up in private collections. Not many of them are left now, and if the illustrations are in good shape – still clear and colourful – even rarer. Not often used for devotional purposes these days, but much coveted by rich men who wish to show their wealth."

I made a record of his comments in my notebook. "And do you think this is most likely what has happened to the missing psalter? Bought for a rich man's collection?" I asked.

"I suspect that is for you to discover," replied Giles gently. "But those who wish to add such a volume to their library and have little scruple about how to obtain it will make their wishes known."

"And has anyone made such wishes known to you?" I asked.

"Has anyone asked me for a Byzantine psalter, you mean?" I nodded, and Giles laughed. "Nicholson's is not that kind of bookseller, Mr Hardiman."

"But you know booksellers who are?" I persisted.

Giles looked more serious. "I hear rumours," he said. We both fell silent.

"And the other two volumes?" I asked eventually.

Giles looked down at the paper in his hands. "Now, the Shakespeare. We have very occasionally come into possession of various early editions, but none as early as this one – the third folio." He looked up at me, his eyes shining. "Interestingly, it contains six additional plays that were thought at the time of printing – 1664, if memory serves – to be by Shakespeare but have since been judged spurious." He frowned slightly in recollection. "One was called *The Puritan Widow*, I believe, and another *A Yorkshire Tragedy*. Oddly, it's much rarer than the second folio, as much of the stock of the third folio was destroyed in the Great Fire of 1666. Your college was extremely lucky to have it – and very unlucky to lose it."

"Would the same sort of collector want both the psalter and the Shakespeare?" I asked.

Giles considered for a moment. "An interesting question," he said. "Possibly – but unlikely. Psalters appeal to those who favour the look of a thing, while the folio is for readers."

"And the third missing book?" I asked.

"Well, some might contend that mathematics combines both," said Giles. "The logic of words and the beauty of pictures."

"I know very little about it," I admitted. "I know enough to stop a trader cheating me, but as for something like this..."

"A first edition of Wallis's *Opera Mathematica*," said the bookseller. "In three volumes."

"And this Wallis is an important mathematician?" I asked.

Giles nodded. "Oh yes. John Wallis. Seventeenth century. He had a particular fondness for deciphering codes. Do you know the symbol for infinity – the figure of eight on its side?" He drew the shape in the air and I nodded. "That was his invention."

"And this *Opera* – it's a collection of his life's work?" I asked.

"That, and some important correspondence between himself and Isaac Newton," Giles looked questioningly at me and I nodded, "and between Newton and a German mathematician called Liebniz, discussing Newton's work on tangents and curves. All that early development of ideas would have been lost without Wallis's determination to see Newton's brilliance recognised. Again, hugely valuable – both academically and financially." He leaned forward and handed the slip of paper back to me, and I tucked it into my notebook. "You know, Mr Hardiman, two things constantly surprise me about college libraries: the richness of their collections, and the carelessness with which they treat them. Perhaps this loss will persuade this college at least to remedy that."

"I should imagine it will," I agreed. "What they – we – are trying to establish is whether these book thefts are connected to other financial misdoings in the college, or whether it is just an unfortunate coincidence. The volumes might simply have been taken by someone connected with the college who covets them, or does not realise their value."

Giles shook his head. "No-one who knew enough about these volumes to want to study them closely would be unaware of their rarity or value," he said firmly. "Ask the librarian at the college if these are three of the most valuable items in their collection. I am almost certain he will confirm that they are, and I fear that you are looking for an adept thief – one who knows exactly where to sell what he has taken."

"And where would that be, in your opinion?" I asked, my pencil poised over my notebook.

"London," said Giles without hesitation. "London in the first instance, then perhaps sold on to buyers on the Continent. I am afraid that books like this might pass through many hands."

"To put distance between the thief and the buyer?" I asked.

"Indeed," said the bookseller, "and everyone wants to take their little slice of profit along the way."

"I hope you don't mind my asking this, Mr Giles," I said, "and I hope you will not take offence, but do you happen to know where I might look in London? Anyone who might have taken the first little slice of profit?"

"I take no offence, sir," said Giles, smiling. "I know my trade, good and bad. Here, pass me your notebook and I will write down a couple of names. There are not many who have the connections for works of this fame and importance."

I did as he asked, then remembered the motto I had jotted into my vocabulary book. I took it out and handed it to him in exchange for my black notebook. "Can you tell me what this means, Mr Giles?" I asked.

"Ah," he said. "So you are talking about St Clement's. I am sorry to learn it. Professor Sandys is a good man and a fine scholar and these losses will pain him."

I could have kicked myself – of course he would recognise it. "I trust that you will not..." I started.

The bookseller held up a hand. "In confidence, Mr Hardiman – no-one shall hear of this from me."

"I am grateful," I said. I pointed at the motto. "I had been meaning to translate it myself, but perhaps you can help."

"Of course," said Giles. "*Dirige nos ad caelum serenum et mare tranquillum.* Guide us to fair skies, well, perhaps fair weather, and calm seas. Very apt, with St Clement being the patron saint of mariners. They will have need of calm seas if they are to ride out this loss."

He handed my vocabulary book back to me and I made to stand, but he put out a hand to stop me.

"Mr Hardiman," he said, "before you go, I have a proposal for you. An opportunity has arisen, and I think you might be just the man to take ideal advantage of it. I was planning to call on you myself to discuss it, but your visit has saved me the walk."

"I am intrigued, Mr Giles," I said, sitting down again.

"Have you heard of the Society for Promoting Useful Knowledge?" he asked. I shook my head. "Perhaps you know it as the Bull Book Club?"

"Ah yes," I said, nodding. "Out at the..." I waved my hand in the general direction of Trumpington Street.

"The Black Bull Inn," confirmed the bookseller. "The book club meets there every Wednesday evening. It has a most acceptable lending library – more than two thousand volumes – and various other items of interest. An orrery, for example – a mechanical model of the planets. A good word for your vocabulary book, Mr Hardiman." He smiled at me. "Membership of the club is limited to fifty men, and, well, not to put too fine a point on it, we have a vacancy. And I am minded to propose you for membership."

My eyebrows shot up. "Me?" I asked.

Giles held up his hand. "It is not entirely the act of charity you may imagine," he said. "There is an admission fee of two pounds and two shillings, and then a quarterly subscription of six shillings. It has been agreed that in certain circumstances the admission fee could be waived – and I would argue strongly that permitting a man on an ostler's wage to join would qualify. But the quarterly subscription must be paid by everyone, and I will quite understand if you feel that it is not how you wish to spend your money. But you are exactly the kind of fellow we would like to have in our club, Mr Hardiman." He leaned forward. "It's not only a library, you see. It's a forum for discussion and the exchange of ideas. Everybody takes his turn to read to the group, we have weekly debates, and anyone can suggest books or instruments that we should add to our collection. You would, I suspect, enjoy spending time with like-minded people." He looked at me intently. "Broad-minded people who value substance above appearance."

Chapter Eleven

CLUB

The room at the Black Bull Inn was already busy and lively with talk by the time Mr Giles and I walked in at ten minutes before the hour. We were puffing slightly from walking up so many stairs; the Society for Promoting Useful Knowledge held its meetings in a room on the top floor of the four-storey building, with another room alongside it furnished as its library. Mr Giles told me that the arrangement had been in place since the establishment of the book club in 1794, and the current innkeeper saw no reason to change things. After all, the book club brought a large number of thirsty men to his premises every Wednesday evening, and the book club's growing reputation lent the Black Bull Inn a certain intellectual respectability that appealed to some travellers.

Just inside the door stood a man of about fifty, what my mother would have called a titty-totty fellow. He barely came up to my shoulder and I'm a compact man. He was dressed in sombre but smart clothes that looked more suited to a London drawing-room than a Cambridge inn, and even from where I stood I could smell his lavender water. "The club president," said Giles under his breath. "Mr Robert Horwood."

"Mr Giles," said the president, nodding in acknowledgement as we drew level with him. "And this must be Mr Hardiman."

I knew that the bookseller had proposed my membership at the previous meeting, including his request that the admission fee be waived, and guessed that the president would have asked around about me. In his place, I would have done the same. And a face like mine was easy to recognise.

"Gregory Hardiman," I confirmed, shaking his hand.

"And I am Robert Horwood. Welcome to the Society for Promoting Useful Knowledge," said Horwood. "I see that Mr Giles has books to return, so he can take you through to the library. The meeting proper will begin at half-past eight, with your election." I must have looked surprised, as Horwood smiled. "Oh yes, it's a foregone conclusion. Mr Giles is one of our most revered members, and in his two decades or more with the club, you are the first new member he has ever proposed. So we listened very carefully to him, and you have been permitted to vault over one or two, shall we say, less interesting nibs waiting to join."

I was uneasy to hear that. "Perhaps I should wait," I said, looking from one man to the other. "I have no wish to take a place that rightfully belongs to someone else."

The bookseller had blushed slightly at being referred to in such complimentary terms. "There are some members," he explained, "who are always quick to nominate someone as soon as a place falls vacant. As Mr Horwood says, I have never nominated anyone before, and so it is me pushing ahead, not you."

"Besides," said Horwood, "you may change your mind about joining when you hear tonight's programme. Mr Sharp is reading an extract from *Melmoth the Wanderer*, to honour the author who died last year. I foresee a lively discussion – I am told that Mr Maturin has some unkind things to say about Roman Catholicism." He shook his head. "But enough from me, Mr Hardiman. Please, go into the library, and I look forward to hearing your five answers."

The bookseller had explained to me that when I was put forward for membership of the club, I would be asked five questions by the president. The answers were a formality, but served as a reminder to all of the aims of the club.

We walked into the library. Around the walls of the room were tall bookcases filled with volumes, with a man on a ladder replacing some on an upper shelf. And in the middle of the room were two low cabinets – presumably containing items like the orrery Giles had mentioned – and a desk at which sat two men, each with a ledger open in front of him.

"There are two librarians," explained Giles. "One on the ladder," he pointed, "and one at the desk. And the other man at the desk is the steward, collecting the quarterly subscriptions that are due. You will take your turn at these duties, as well as serving as president. The office-holders change every quarter. I myself will serve as president from next month. See: members are returning the items they have borrowed, and checking out new ones." He indicated the two books he was carrying. "Come: I will return these, and then we can choose what we are to borrow this week. You cannot yet officially borrow anything, but I can take up to six and I can never read more than two in the week, so you can have some of my allocation. As long as you return them on time – I won't be held responsible for your late fines."

In my room later that evening, I burnt the candle right down as I looked at the two books Giles had borrowed for me and reflected on the interesting evening I had spent with, as promised, like-minded people. The library was a treasure trove of tempting books but in the end I had chosen John Aikin's collection of letters on poetry that he had written to a young lady named Mary, and a collection of poems by Thomas Gray. On Giles's advice, I had made a note in the back of my vocabulary book of other volumes that had caught my eye, so that I could find them quickly in the future.

My election to membership had indeed been a formality – I was told that there were no balls at all cast against me – but the questions had been put to me in a solemn manner, and I had answered them likewise. And my answers were truthful, I can assure you. I confirmed that I had no particular disrespect for any of the members of the club, and that I did not think that anyone should be harmed in any way for his opinions or form of worship. I declared that I loved mankind in general, of whatever profession or religion. Finally, I promised to love truth for its own sake, and to endeavour to find it myself and communicate it to others. I was then welcomed into the Bull Book Club with a round of applause. The ongoing subscription would require me to sacrifice elsewhere, but it is surely better for any man to pour money into his education rather than down his throat. And with that thought, I shook my second tablet of the day from its little brown bottle and ruefully swallowed it.

Chapter Twelve

BANKER

I was at my second meeting of the Bull Book Club and this time I had gone alone; Geoffrey Giles's father had come down with a chill and Giles had stayed at home to care for him. Thankfully the other members were as welcoming as Mr Giles, and several of them nodded at me as I queued to return my books. Just as I turned away from the desk, a voice hailed me from across the room.

"I thought it was you, Hardiman."

I turned to see who was addressing me.

"Mr Fisher," I said, with genuine pleasure. George Fisher was the youngest son of a banking family, and everyone in Cambridge knew that he stood in the professional shadow of his father and his older brother. But he outstripped them both in charm and good nature, and I liked him very much. Tall and lean, with an angular face, long nose and dark eyebrows and hair, he was a handsome man, and I understood that several good Cambridge families had their eye on him for their daughters.

"I have been in London for a month," he said as we went into the other room to find seats for the evening's business. "I had no idea you had joined our book club – it will be all the better for it, as I've rarely known a man talk more sense."

"You flatter me, sir," I said.

"Nonsense," said Fisher, waving amiably at other members as we settled into our seats. "That discussion we had about the welfare of coaching inn horses has stayed with me."

"Mrs Bird had a word with me about that," I admitted. "She said I should not be boring customers with my opinions."

"Then more fool Mrs Bird," said the banker stoutly. "If a customer asks a question about horses and the ostler has something sensible to say, then he should say it. Ah, here we go: Mr Williams is in the chair, so we're in for a long evening."

Mr Fisher was not wrong: the reader was fond of the sound of his own voice, and no amount of coughing or shifting by his audience could persuade him to hurry. But eventually, just as the clock of Great St Mary's was chiming half-past ten, we made our escape. We all trooped down the several flights of stairs and emerged into the cold night, people shaking hands and calling farewell as they set off in various directions. Fisher turned left, heading towards his home on Petty Cury.

"May I walk with you?" I asked. "You once asked my view on horses and now I would like to ask your view on financial matters."

"By all means," said Fisher, "although my father would be astonished to know that anyone considered my view on financial matters worth hearing."

"It's a rather delicate situation," I said.

"It often is, when money is concerned," observed Fisher.

"Indeed," I agreed. "One of the colleges – I cannot tell you which one – has lost some valuable items. And I have agreed to ask around to see what I can uncover."

"They have been burgled, you mean?" asked the banker.

We crossed Trumpington Street and turned into Bene't Street.

"Not in the traditional sense, no," I replied. "No-one broke in at dead of night. But nonetheless, certain items are no longer where they should be. And I wondered whether you, or perhaps another banking house in town, had heard of someone coming into money unexpectedly."

"Ah," said Fisher. "A windfall."

"If you will," I said. "I did not mention it to the Master, but it occurred to me that perhaps the items were chosen not so much for their value but more because they would not be missed – or at least, not straight away. So it seems that the thief knew the ways of the college."

"One of the fellows, you think?" asked the banker. "Or a member of the college staff?"

I shrugged. "It's possible," I said. "But before I mention it to the Master – after all, it's quite an accusation – I want to be more sure of my ground."

"Very wise," agreed Fisher.

We stepped smartly into the road as a drunken man tumbled from the doorway of the Eagle. He got to his feet, replaced his hat with careful dignity, and tottered off, one hand on the wall to steady himself.

"If you are thinking of that sort of involvement," continued the banker as we started off again, "have you considered the bursar?"

"Why would you suggest the bursar?" I asked.

"In my experience," said Fisher, "bursars are nominally in charge of college finances but generally have very little interest in them. You see, when most of the colleges were founded, the bursar's responsibilities were limited: he was required to supervise the collection of rents from college properties and manage expenditure, usually by approving invoices presented by the butler, cook and so on. Both sides of the equation were largely unchanging, and could be managed in very little time by anyone with a very little knowledge. But in recent years," he looked in both directions as we walked across Butcher Row, "things have grown more complicated."

"Complicated?" I asked. "In what way?"

"Colleges now have many more ways to invest their money, and as they expand and admit more scholars, they have more need of profit. Instead of simply buying land and properties as they did in the past, they are now investing in bonds and shares – and buying and selling them more frequently. In other words, a bursar must now know how to manage not only real estate, but also financial assets – and how to keep an eye on those assets. This is more time-consuming and requires additional skills and, to be frank, many bursars are not up to the job."

We turned into Petty Cury. It surprised me that the Fishers still lived above their bank in this cramped, untidy street when their money could have bought them a fine house on the edge of town, but then I suppose bankers do not become wealthy by lavishing their money on fancy lodgings.

"Then why do the colleges tolerate them?" I asked. "Why not pass on the responsibility to someone who knows about modern finance?"

"Do you know how much a bursar is paid?" asked Fisher by way of reply.

I smiled. "Actually, I think I do. I have been told it's about twenty pounds a year."

Fisher smiled in return. "And you've been told right, Mr Hardiman. For that money, nobody wants the job these days – not with the additional time and skills it requires. Some colleges have considered forcing their fellows to take the post in rotation, but then you end up with a succession of resentful novices. Those who do take it on tend to stay put because there is no-one willing to take over from them – one I know has been doing the job for more than twenty years." I nodded, thinking of John Galpin at St Clement's.

"And I should imagine that concerns you as it does me," I said as we stopped outside the bank.

"And why do you say that?" asked Fisher.

"Well," I chose my words carefully – after all, college bursars would almost certainly be among the bank's clients. "If you have a man who holds a position for many years, a position that no-one else wants, and a position in which he is almost expected to do poorly, might that not be the perfect hiding place for a man who wishes to..." Here my imagination failed me and I could not think of a polite way to phrase it.

"Line his own pocket?" suggested the banker. I nodded. Fisher looked at me levelly then held out his hand for me to shake. "Have you heard of William Wood?" he asked. I shook my head. "Well, it might be useful for you to know about him. But not this evening, Mr Hardiman." The banker yawned and covered his mouth with the back of his hand. "Allow me a little time to look out the details and I will come to see you."

CHAPTER THIRTEEN

SCANDAL

George Fisher was as good as his word. I had just finished settling the horses from the *Telegraph* when he appeared in the stables the next evening.

"Mr Hardiman," he said. "If you still want to know about William Wood, I have some time now. I have told my brother that I am calling on potential clients, and he is happy just to see me out of the bank."

I knew that Fisher's brother Thomas was more than ten years older than him, and his reputation around town was as a serious, perhaps even dull, man. I could well imagine that he and his lively younger brother might find working together something of a mutual trial.

"I am grateful, sir," I said, checking each door through habit as we walked back through the stables. The animals were quiet, enjoying their food before settling for the night. "If you're thirsty we can go indoors, or if you would prefer more privacy, we can go up to the loft."

"The loft?" repeated Fisher, looking amused. "I had no idea you had a little eyrie, Hardiman."

It was my turn to repeat. "An eyrie?" I asked. "What is that?" I took out my vocabulary book and pencil.

Fisher watched as I wrote – he was familiar with my word-collecting. "E, Y," he started. "No, Y, R, I… here, let me." He took the book from me and wrote the word before passing the pencil to me again. "It means a nest for a bird of prey, like an eagle – built high up in a tree, or on a cliff or mountainside."

I made a note of it and put the book away. "I do so like words," I said. "As you must love numbers, I suppose, being a banker."

"Hah!" said Fisher. "I am a banker by birth, not by inclination. We Fishers have been bankers in Cambridge for generations – as you will hear in a moment – but some of us are better suited to it than others. Up here?" He pointed up the ladder.

"You go on up," I said. "I will fetch some coffee for us from the kitchen."

When I returned with a small tray, which I balanced carefully as I climbed the ladder, Fisher had settled into one of the two chairs. I put the coffee pot and two mugs onto the crate that I used as a table, and reached into my pocket for the napkin containing the two slices of walnut loaf that I had coaxed from the new cook. Fisher poured our drinks and then settled back in his chair, coffee in one hand and walnut loaf in the other.

"It's snug in here," he said approvingly, through a mouthful of cake. "Much more comfortable than our apartment in Petty Cury."

"I find that hard to believe," I said. "I doubt you are sharing space with horse fodder." I nodded towards the sacks stored under the eaves.

"More to my taste, then," he amended. "My brother's wife is from Ireland – a country girl, from a simple home. And to make up for it she has stuffed her marital home with more furniture than you would think possible. Every seat in the place is covered in some dainty, slippery stuff which exists only to repel all boarders. As for allowing me to drink from a mug and eat a slice of cake without a plate..." He grinned at me like a schoolboy, then looked around him. "But you don't live here, do you?" he asked.

I shook my head. "I have lodgings in a house out along Jesus Lane," I said. "Mr Bird – the innkeeper – said I could live in if I wanted, but I like my own place. My privacy."

"I envy you," said Fisher. "My father won't hear of me moving out." We sat in comfortable silence for a few moments. The banker put the last piece of walnut loaf into his mouth and licked his fingers. "Well, now: William Wood," he said. I took out my notebook. "Wood was admitted to St John's College as a sizar in 1764. Don't be impressed that I know the date – I checked before coming to see you, and I have written down the key facts in case I forget them." He patted his pocket.

"A sizar?" I asked.

"S, I, Z, A, R," said the banker. "A poor scholar who is given board, lodging and tuition at a college in exchange for performing various duties – waiting at table and the like. Wood was the son of a farmer. He showed just enough brains to matriculate, but four years later he took the wooden spoon in the mathematical tripos – that means he came last of all the students. He turned his attention to the church and became deacon then priest then vicar in various places. In 1775 – when he was about thirty – he applied for a fellowship at St John's. He lost out, quite fairly, to another chap, but Wood was something of a trouble-maker and he made such a stink about it that the college eventually booted the other chap out of his rooms and installed William Wood instead." Fisher paused and lifted his mug – finding it empty, he refilled it from the pot and took a sip. He then took a sheet of paper from his pocket, read it quickly and continued. "In March 1789 he was appointed junior bursar. As you now know, it is not a popular responsibility, and doubtless he faced little opposition when he put his name forward.

Six years later he became senior bursar, with almost total control over the college finances."

"I have a feeling that this is not going to end well for the college," I said. "Putting the worst mathematics scholar in Cambridge in charge of the money."

"Ha!" said Fisher. "And you are right: Wood speculated with college money by giving it to relatives of his to invest, and those relatives lost everything when the bank holding their assets collapsed. Speculating with college money was unwise, and entrusting it to his own relatives rather than to an objective third party was foolish, but there it is. Within two years he had lost almost all of the college's money."

"How did he lay hands on the money to give it to his relatives?" I asked. "Surely it wasn't just lying around – wasn't it in a bank?"

Fisher looked at me approvingly. "Now then, that question alone shows more financial astuteness than most college masters ever exhibit. When Wood was at St John's, the rules were different, well, actually there weren't any rules. College money was held with very few safeguards. But in 1802, seeing the difficulties that St John's had had with Wood, the University passed an order requiring college monies to be deposited in a bank account, with the interest on that account to be shared among the college officers. The thinking, I suppose, was that a professional banker would offer guidance and care, and that if the money was removed by the bursar, the other college officers would notice that they weren't receiving any interest payments and would question him."

"And what happened to Wood?" I asked.

"Well, he was bagged in the spring of 1797 and instructed to answer questions about his activities – he dragged his feet and supplied unsatisfactory answers, and was asked to move out of college. He made representations to all sorts of people, including the Bishop of Ely, and – hoping to mollify him – the college set him up as rector of Lawford in Essex in," he checked the paper again, "1806. By this time he was no longer in Cambridge, and for good reason: he had fled to the Isle of Man to avoid being arrested by agents of the college's banker – one Mr William Fisher."

"William Fisher?" I repeated. "Your ancestor?"

"Indeed," said the banker. "Sadly, there is no evidence that William managed to bring Mr Wood to justice. Wood simply disappears from college life and records, and died at his sister's house in London in 1821 – still earning money from his Lawford living."

"And all bursars in Cambridge will be aware of the story of William Wood, do you think?" I asked.

"I'm sure the story has travelled to Oxford too," said Fisher with a smile.

"And so a bursar looking to line his own pockets would have to be more careful – more devious?" I suggested.

"I should imagine so," replied Fisher. "College masters are more aware of the dangers now, and certainly all the local bankers will be alert to another scandal. No-one wants to be implicated in another college losing its money. St John's lost about £5,000 thanks to Wood's mismanagement, and they are still working to claw it back."

Chapter Fourteen

Wine

I was sweeping the yard after the departure of the *Wisbech Day* when in through the gate came a young man pushing two wooden crates on a barrow. He nodded at me and headed towards the kitchen. He halted the barrow, lifted one of the crates with a grunt, and turned to the kitchen door, realising just too late that with both hands holding the crate he could not open it. He shot a despairing look at me, leaning backwards slightly to balance the weight of the crate. I trotted across the yard and opened the door for him, holding it while he took in the first crate and then returned with an empty one, which he used to prop open the kitchen door. I could see that the second crate waiting on the barrow was full of bottles.

"Thank you, sir," he said. "I'll just take in this second lot."

"Shut that blasted door!" yelled the cook from inside the kitchen, and I winked at the lad.

"We'd better do as he says," I suggested. "You take in that full crate and I'll wheel the barrow out of the way for you."

He returned a few minutes later with a second empty crate. He put it on the barrow and then took his order book from the pocket of his apron and checked it. He held it out to me.

"Does that look like Bird to you?" he asked.

I peered at the signature. "Just about," I said.

"Mr Barker is very particular," he said. "If I don't get the customer's signature on the order, he says, and the customer says he didn't receive what he ordered, he'll take it from my wages. Not that he pays me enough to pay for a bottle, let alone a crate."

"Mr Barker, the wine merchant on Market Hill?" I asked.

The young man closed the order book and shoved it back into his pocket.

"That's him," he said. "Only a year older than me, but full of himself now that he's in charge. His old man died last year."

We heard footsteps on the stairs leading down from the gallery of rooms around the yard and both turned to look. It was one of the maids, carrying a mop and bucket.

"Mr Hardiman," she said, nodding at me.

"Agnes," I replied. "Allow me," and I stepped forward to open the kitchen door for her. She glanced at the lad from Barker's, tossed her head a little and gave a half-smile before disappearing into the kitchen with a swish of her hips.

I looked at my companion. He was staring at the kitchen door, his mouth slightly open and his arms hanging at his sides. He blinked a couple of times. Love – or maybe its unruly cousin lust – had just clouted him round the head. Poor devil.

"Mr..." I said, and then repeated it. "Mr..."

He shook his head to clear it. "Grantham," he said, still looking at the kitchen door. "Charlie Grantham."

"Well, Mr Grantham," I said, "I have a proposal for you. I need a bit of information about the wine business, and if you can see your way to supplying it, then I don't see why I shouldn't have a word with Miss Agnes. Tell her what a fine fellow you are, good prospects and so on. She listens to me, does Agnes." To be honest, I knew Agnes no better than I knew any of the maids at the Sun, which is to say not at all, but all I was offering was to speak to the girl. Whether she chose to listen, well, that was her business.

Charlie Grantham looked at me. "What sort of information?" he asked, narrowing his eyes.

"Nothing to get you into trouble," I said, raising both my hands in surrender. "The thing is, Mr Grantham, I need someone with your expertise, your understanding of the wine business to help me on a very important matter for the coroner."

"The coroner?" he said with surprise.

I nodded, leaning towards him. "A good and decent man has been killed, Charlie, and I am trying to help his widow. And I think it has something to do with stealing food and drink from colleges and selling it on."

Charlie indicated the empty crates. "Drink like this, you mean?"

I shrugged. "That's why I need you, Charlie."

He thought for a moment, looking towards the kitchen door again. "And you'd put in a good word for me with Agnes?" I nodded. "What do you need to know?" he asked.

Chapter Fifteen

PEONIES

As I can remember only too clearly from those thrilling days when I first knew Lucia, a young man with his eye on a young woman finds untapped stores of energy and determination. And so it was only three days later that I was beckoned into the kitchen by Poor Jamie.

"I've to tell you something, Mr Hardiman," he said. He walked over to his spot by the sink, and jerked his head to indicate that I should follow. "It's a secret, Mr Hardiman," he said, dropping his voice.

"Are you sure you should tell me, then, Jamie?" I asked gently.

He looked at me, nodding emphatically. "Not a secret from you, Mr Hardiman," he said earnestly. "It's a secret for you."

"Well, in that case, Jamie," I said, "I'm all ears." He looked at me and frowned. "I mean that I'm listening very carefully," I explained.

"It's a secret from Charlie – Charlie with the bottles," he said.

"Charlie Grantham?" I asked.

Jamie shrugged. "He brings the bottles on a barrow," he continued. "He's nice to me. Sometimes he gives me a barley twist." The fellow's eyes lit up at the memory of the sweet treat. I had my suspicions that Charlie was being nice to Jamie in hopes of impressing Agnes and the other maids, but still, a kindness is always welcome.

"And what did Charlie ask you to tell me?" I asked.

"He said," and Jamie closed his eyes, the better to remember the right words, "he said he has what you want and you're to meet him at the Greyhound at six o'clock."

"Thank you, Jamie," I said. "You remembered that perfectly – you have been a great help. Now," I dug into the pocket of my coat, "it's not a barley twist, but would you like a Pontefract cake?" I held out the brown paper bag and nodded at him. He delicately dipped his hand into the bag and picked out one of the black discs. "It's strong, mind," I said as he popped it into his mouth. His eyes widened as he sucked.

"Strong," he mumbled as he chewed, "but good."

"Just like you, eh, Jamie?" I said, offering him the bag again.

I could well understand why Charlie Grantham had chosen the Greyhound for our meeting. Heading out of town on St Andrew's Street, just past the Spinning House, it was not the sort of establishment where he was likely to encounter his employer or any of his customers. In short, the Greyhound was a cut-throat inn. At six o'clock it was full of men – some downing a quick drink before they headed home, others settling in for the evening because they had nowhere better to go. I gave my eyes a moment to adjust to the gloom and then spotted Charlie beckoning to me from a small table in the corner of the smoke-filled room. I elbowed my way through and Charlie retrieved for me the stool that he had hidden under the table. Spying a new customer, the innkeeper called at our table on his way to the counter and we ordered two tankards.

They appeared almost instantly and we both took a sip. Charlie grimaced and wiped his mouth.

"That's poor stuff," he observed.

"I daresay you know a sight more about drink these days," I said. "How long have you worked for Mr Barker?"

He paused to think. "Three years this midsummer," he replied. "The old Mr Barker took me on." He took another sip and then pushed the tankard from him. "Things were different then."

"In what way?" I asked.

"He was a proper man of business," said Charlie, choosing his words carefully. "He had a lot of respect, and some good customers in the town and at the University."

"And his son does not?" I asked.

Charlie shifted in his seat, leaning forwards. I did likewise.

"Old Mr Barker died suddenly," he said. "His son had only been working with him for a few months, and he's not a man to take instruction or advice, so he had not learned much. He was only twenty-five when he took over, and he has brought another man – Mr Eaden – into the business. Mr Eaden is my age, Mr Hardiman. And knows even less about the trade." He sighed. "The business no longer has a steady hand on the tiller, and if I can see it, so can everyone else."

"Everyone else?" I asked.

Charlie shook his head. "I've already said too much," he said. "If Mr Barker heard that I had been talking about him..."

"Peonies," I said. "Agnes likes peonies, especially the pale pink ones with the yellow centres. And lemon drops from Mr Byford's shop on Bene't Street. And..." I stopped and smiled at him. "But perhaps that is enough for now. It wouldn't do to tell you when her next half-day is, or where she and her sister will be walking that day."

He gave me a long look and then made up his mind. "The old Mr Barker never let anyone except the colleges have anything on tick," he said. "The colleges paid their accounts every six months, of course, but for everyone else it was full payment on delivery. But the young Mr Barker and Mr Eaden said we were old-fashioned, that modern businesses offer credit to everyone. You saw me with the account book the other day." I nodded. "All I got that day was a signature – no payment. Now, Mr Bird is probably good for the money, but plenty aren't – and we're getting more and more customers macing us." He dropped his voice. "We're losing money fast, Mr Hardiman. Despite..."

"Despite what, Mr Grantham?" I asked.

Charlie closed his eyes for a moment and shook his head then took a deep breath. "They are cheating the colleges," he said in a rush. "They charge the colleges for more than they are delivering – sometimes just a bit more, sometimes twice as much. I know it's not right, Mr Hardiman, but my mother and little brothers need my wages. I'm looking for another job, so if you hear of anything." He looked pleadingly at me.

"I will certainly do what I can for you, Mr Grantham," I said, and I meant it. I lifted my tankard to drain it and changed my mind – Charlie was right when he called it poor stuff. I stood and held out my hand for him to shake. "Thursday afternoon," I said. "And they're planning to walk to Grantchester, if the weather is fine."

Chapter Sixteen

DESTINATIONS

It was time for me to learn more about John Galpin, the spider at the centre of the college's web of finances. I decided to find the Bursar where he spent most of his time: the Philosophical Society. According to Geoffrey Giles, the society had been founded about five years earlier by three men of science – a geologist, a botanist and a mineralogist (three more interesting words for my vocabulary book) – in order to promote the study of natural history. They rented a good-sized building in Bridge Street to house their growing library and museum and to hold lectures, and had soon added a reading room where members could socialise and read the latest newspapers and scientific journals. Apparently Mr Galpin spent several hours every day in that reading room, and so I positioned myself in Dolphin Lane, where I could see the Society's door and hopefully have a word with the Bursar on his way in or out. With his Anglesey leg (the result of a childhood coach accident, according to Giles), he would be easy to spot.

And indeed, about ten minutes later, I heard the unmistakable clapping sound of a jointed wooden leg coming along Sidney Street. I was about to walk to waylay Galpin at the door of the Philosophical Society when I heard him come to a halt – or rather, his wooden leg stopped making its distinctive noise. "What do you want?" I heard him say, in a none too friendly tone. I strained my ears but could not make out the answer, although I could tell that the two men were arguing. After a few moments, their disagreement grew louder.

"And I told you that would be an end of it," said Galpin.

"If you think a nib like you has any sway in my world, you are much mistaken," said his opponent. "As you will soon find to your cost."

I heard footsteps heading away from me and poked my head round the corner. All I could see was the back of a man walking away up Sidney Street, while Galpin was leaning against the wall with one hand while holding the other to his chest. I walked towards him as though by chance.

"Are you unwell, sir?" I asked.

The Bursar stood up straight, pausing to get his balance. "No, I am quite well, sir," he said. "Thank you for your concern."

I tipped my hat to him and walked on. Something was bothering me, something that the other man had said to him. But I just could not get hold of it.

I looked back, expecting to see the Bursar going into the Philosophical Society, but instead he was walking away from me along Jesus Lane. I was curious to see where he would go, after being threatened like that, and I turned to follow him at a safe distance. Thanks to the clapping of his wooden leg I was able to let him get some way ahead of me without fear of losing him, and he kept up a smart pace. We went all the way along Jesus Lane, past Mrs Jacobs' house, and then struck out across Butt's Green. The Bursar walked determinedly along the footpath towards the Fort St George.

The inn sat alongside the sluice, and Galpin walked past the inn and onto the waterside, heading for the small shed set up there by the Union Steam Packet company, if the sign above the door was to be believed. He spoke to a man in the shed, handed him something, and then left. I ducked behind a tree and watched the Bursar walking back towards town.

I made my own way to the little shed. Sitting inside was a man smoking a pipe and reading a newspaper, his grubby fingers tracing the words as he read. He looked up as I approached and sighed mightily.

"Does no-one read the sign?" he asked, pointing with the stem of his pipe to the notice stuck alongside the door. "Monday and Friday mornings at nine o'clock. And today is..." He looked at me, his head tilted to one side. "Today is Tuesday," he finished, as though speaking to a very dull-witted child. He shook his head. "A town full of scholars, and you can't read a simple sign."

I waited until he had blown himself out. "I am not here for the packet to Lynn," I said.

"In that case, you're in the wrong place," he said, and turned back to his newspaper.

"I am here to ask a question," I continued.

"And I am here to sell tickets for the Lynn packet, not to answer questions," he said, and reached up to close the door.

I put my foot against it. "Might you sell an answer?" I asked. That caught his attention. "If you're willing, I might forget to mention to the owners of the Union Steam Packet Company that their ticket seller sits in a wooden shed on a wooden dock smoking his pipe, which is against the rules of his employment." It was a guess, but it hit the mark. He looked uncomfortable. I reached into my pocket and pulled out a few coins and inspected them in the palm of my hand.

"What do you want to know?" he asked.

"A few minutes ago a man with a wooden leg was here. He spoke to you. What did he want?" I asked.

"He wanted to know the whereabouts of someone who works on the packet," he said.

I selected a shilling and gave it to him. He turned it over to check it and then tucked it into the pocket of his waistcoat. I jingled the remaining coins in my palm.

"He gave you something," I said. "What did he give you?"

"A letter," he said, eyeing the remaining coins in my hand.

I picked out another shilling and held it up. "Who is the letter for?" I asked.

"The man who works on the packet," he said, as though it were obvious. I handed over the shilling; it joined the other one in the waistcoat pocket.

"And can I see the letter?" I asked.

His eyes flicked to mine and back to the coins. I turned over a couple of them and let my fingers come to rest on a silver half-crown. He thought for a moment and then opened a drawer in his little desk and took out a folded letter. "You can't keep it, mind," he said. "Half a crown to read it." We made our exchange – coin for letter – and I returned the rest of the coins to my pocket.

I looked at the letter: it was addressed to a Mr Muncie. I unfolded the paper and read it. "Sir, we cannot delay," it said. "All remaining items must go with you on Friday. I will see you on Thursday as planned – please make arrangements for carriage. Yours, JG."

"And this Mr Muncie," I said, folding the letter and handing it back to the ticket seller. "What does he look like?"

"Half a crown," said the ticket seller.

I shook my head. "A shilling," I said. "I have to eat, you know."

"I daresay," he replied, holding out his hand. "A shilling it is, then." I paid. "Older than you, younger than me. About your height, but fatter. Ginger hair."

As I left the riverside, I looked at the schedule for the steam packet and knew what I had to do.

The porter barely looked up as I passed; he simply waved in greeting as I walked towards Mr Vaughan's rooms. The footman explained that the Master was out of college at a meeting of the Heads of House but that he would return within the hour and I was welcome to wait. With the shelves of books at my disposal, I would have been happy to wait all afternoon, but I had only an hour until I had to be back at the stables to prepare the coach for Bury St Edmunds.

I was lost in the riches of an atlas when the Master returned. He walked over to the table to see what I had been reading.

"Ah," he said. "The *Atlas Universalis.* Meant for use in schools, but I look at it more often than almost any other book in my collection. Look, here," he turned some pages, "this is my favourite map. The Arctic Frozen Sea and Russian Tartary – what an adventure that would be! Or this," he turned a few more pages, "New Holland, as they called it."

"I have been there," I said, "and a Dutchman I knew said it bore no resemblance at all to his homeland."

The Master looked at me in astonishment. "You have been to Australia?" he asked.

"With my regiment," I explained. "The 48th Northamptonshire. I was there for seven years. New South Wales. On convict guard duty."

"That must have been tough work," he said. "Those poor souls."

“Some were more deserving of our pity than others,” I replied. I looked back at the atlas and put my finger on the map. “There: that’s where we were garrisoned.” I pointed at Port Jackson.

“Fascinating,” said the Master. “You must tell me about it. But not today: my man tells me that you are due back at the Sun very soon. So how can I help you? Have you news of our missing property?”

“Perhaps,” I said. “It may be that it is being sent from Cambridge to Lynn, and then – I assume – to the Continent. I will know more in a few days’ time, but I am afraid I must ask you for some money. Not for me,” I added quickly, “but to pay people to find information for me. I gave a few shillings to a man today, which is how I know about the Lynn route. And now I am going to ask someone I know – a coach driver – to do some work for me in Lynn, and I will need to pay him for his time.”

“Of course, of course,” said Vaughan, walking over to his desk. “I should have thought of it myself – please forgive me.” He opened one of the desk drawers and took out a small wooden box. From it he counted out some coins and held them out to me. “Would that suffice for now?” he asked.

“It would,” I replied, taking the coins. “I will keep a record of what I spend.”

“Thank you, Mr Hardiman,” he said. “You are a good friend to St Clement’s.”

Chapter Seventeen

Union

The landlord of the Black Bull looked surprised when I walked in.

"Mr Hardiman?" he said, glancing at the clock on the wall. "You are rather early for the book club."

I put my hand on the counter for a moment to catch my breath – I had all but run across town, as I did not have long between my own duties at the Sun.

"Forgive me," I said, panting slightly. "I'm not as trim as I should be. Is Will Morris in the yard?"

"The driver of the *Union*?" asked the landlord. I nodded. He looked again at the clock. "You've about fifteen minutes until he's due to leave," he said. "If I know Will, he'll be in the kitchen, cadging supplies from the cook. Through that door, along the corridor and it's the last on the right."

I raised a hand in thanks and followed his directions. As he had predicted, the coach driver was in the kitchen, loading his satchel with edibles for the journey.

"Gregory Hardiman," he said warmly when he saw me. He held out his hand and I shook it. "It's been a while."

"It has indeed, Will," I replied. "I have a favour to ask of you, but..." I jerked my head to indicate the cook with his back to us.

Will raised an eyebrow. "A favour, eh?" he said. "You can tell me about it in the yard. And while we're at it you can give me your opinion of the horses."

We walked out into the yard, which was similar to that of the Sun but slightly larger. The *Union* was being readied for departure; a lad was washing the last of the grime from the doors, and one porter was scrambling over the coach like a monkey while another handed him bags and packages to be stowed in any available space.

"Well now," said Morris, reaching up to put his satchel behind the foot-board. "This favour of yours."

"Favour is perhaps the wrong word," I said. "More of a paid errand, if you will."

"Paid, you say?" said the driver. "Well, I'm not going to say no to being up in the stirrups for once." He looked at me sharply. "Nothing on the cross, is it?"

I shook my head. "But it will take a bit of time, which is why I thought of you. Tell me, Will: do you still have your young lady in Lynn?"

"I do," said Morris, the corners of his mouth turning up.

"And do you still have that arrangement with the other driver, so that you can stay a few nights with her?" I continued.

"I do," said Morris.

I am sure the driver's domestic arrangements will amuse you as they did me when I first heard of them. Will is a married man, with a wife and kids in London. But he has a great fondness for female company, and he and another driver have cooked up a clever scheme. Will drives the *Union* to Lynn on a Wednesday, but instead of driving it back again to London on the Thursday, he swaps with another driver who does that run. The second driver brings the coach back to Lynn on the Friday, and Will returns with it on Saturday – gaining himself a three-night stay in Lynn with his young lady. Mrs Morris has apparently never thought to question the coach timetable – or perhaps her husband's frequent absences suit her as well. Whatever the marital implications, Will's sojourn in Lynn would be very useful to me.

"Well, while you are in Lynn," I continued, "I need you to look out for something for me." The driver raised an eyebrow. "Someone," I corrected myself. "There will be some goods arriving in Lynn on Friday evening, on the steam packet from here, carried by a Mr Muncie. A man of middling years, about my height but heavier, with red hair. And I need to know where he goes with them and what he does with them."

"What sort of goods?" asked Morris.

"I'm not entirely certain," I admitted, "but they will be valuable, and probably quite small – taken from their rightful owner and destined for sale on the Continent, we're assuming."

Just then the ostler brought out the first pair of horses and backed them into the traces. He saw me and nodded, his eyes narrowed. Morris cocked his head at the horses and I went to have a closer look, running my hand over each animal's back and then down its legs, one at a time. The horses stamped and shook their heads, jingling the harness. The second pair was then brought out and harnessed in front, and I made the same inspection. The ostler watched me with his arms crossed.

"This one," I said, pointing at one of the rear horses, "is reluctant to put weight on the offside hind leg – keep an eye on that. Otherwise, they are healthy beasts." As if to agree, one of the front horses lifted his tail and dropped a generous pile of manure onto the cobbles.

"Hah!" said Morris, readying himself to climb onto his bench. "That has lightened the load, at least." He shook my hand. "I shall see you on Saturday, then. We're due in at one o'clock."

"I'll be here," I said.

Chapter Eighteen

RESULTS

Although I did not have to be back at the Sun to see the *Wisbech Day* off to St Ives until half-past two, I was so keen to hear what Will Morris had found that I had my midday snack early and was waiting in the street outside the Black Bull from half-past twelve. There was plenty to see: with several colleges, a number of inns and the hospital along its length, Trumpington Street is never quiet. At ten minutes to the hour I heard the halloo of a coach driver, and I pressed myself against the wall as I watched Will turn his horses and the *Union* expertly into the yard. He brought the coach to a halt, tied up the ribbons and jumped down, handing me his satchel as he made a dash for the privy.

"Ah, that's better," he said when he returned.

"Good journey?" I asked, passing back his satchel.

"Fair enough," he said. "Come on: you can buy me a drink."

We settled ourselves at a small table in the parlour and the pot boy brought over two tankards without being asked.

Will took a long draught and wiped the back of his hand across his mouth. "You were right about that horse," he said. "Went lame just this side of Ely."

"I'm sorry to hear it," I said.

Will shook his head. "The ostler at the Bull in Ely is a good fellow," he said. "He takes nearly as much care of the animals as you do. Nearly." He winked at me. "Now," he reached down for his satchel and unbuckled it, taking out a folded piece of paper, "you'll be wanting to know about Mr Muncie." He smoothed the paper out on the table. "I wrote it all down, as you're paying. I made sure I was waiting at the Common Staithe yesterday evening when the packet arrived – I saw it tie up. There were only three passengers: two women, looked like mother and daughter, and Mr Muncie. Just as you said: red hair, with a belly on him. He had five things with him: a small leather bag which he kept, and then four packages that he passed on to someone he met on the staithe."

"What did the four packages look like?" I asked. "And what did he look like, the man Muncie met?"

Will held up a hand. "I told you," he said, laughing and tapping the paper with his finger. "I wrote it all down. All the packages were wrapped in cloth and tied with string – carefully done, I'd say. It was hard to be certain from where I was sitting, but I think there were wax seals. Two of the packages were large and flat."

"Like pictures?" I suggested. "Paintings?"

"Very possibly," agreed Will. "The other two were much smaller, fatter. About this size." He held out his hands.

"Ornaments, then," I said. "Books, perhaps?"

He shook his head. "Not flat enough for books – more lumpy."

I thought of the paintings that the Master had described to me, and the statue of the kneeling angel. And a fourth item, perhaps from another college.

"And the man who met Muncie?" I asked.

"Ah now," Will smiled at me mischievously. "Did I say it was a man?"

I raised an eyebrow. "A woman?"

The driver nodded. "I think they knew each other, but not well. Not in that way." He opened his eyes wide, and I knew what he meant and I believed him. After all, he was something of an expert on relations between men and women. "More's the pity for him, I should say – she was an elegant piece. Tall, well-dressed, hair just so. If I had to hazard a guess, I'd say she was not an Englishwoman. French perhaps. I've had one or two in the coach before now, and there's something about them. Self-contained. Confident. And this woman, she was like that."

"So if we take another look at what you saw," I said, leafing back through the notes I had been taking, "there was Mr Muncie – red-haired and with a belly. And then there was a mysterious Frenchwoman: elegant, tall, neat hair, self-contained and confident."

Will chuckled. "If you could choose between a fat Englishman and a comely Frenchwoman, who would you look at more carefully?"

"Did your interest extend to overhearing a name, or anything they said to each other?" I asked.

He shook his head. "After they had completed their business, I watched Muncie walk to the Crown and Mitre. The woman headed towards the town and I followed her until she went into the Duke's Head Hotel. I returned to both establishments and had a word. I had to palm the two lads I spoke to..." He looked at me questioningly.

"Of course," I said. "You will not be out of pocket."

"Muncie bought a ticket to return to Cambridge on the next packet, which left this morning," he said. "And our Mademoiselle told the hotel staff that she would be leaving the next day – that's today – on a boat for Antwerp."

"Flanders," I said.

"Yes," said Will, "but it turns out that there are no passenger boats travelling between Lynn and Flanders. Only commercial services. So for her to be on one of them, she would have to be married to a captain, or at least passing as his wife." He picked up his tankard, drained it and put it back on the table. "And that is that," he said, folding up the paper he had written on and handing it to me, "apart from the small matter of my payment."

"You have been very helpful, Will," I said, reaching into my pocket. "This is for you," I counted out his money from the coins the Master had given me, "and this is to repay what you gave the two lads."

"I'll be in my wife's good books tonight," he said, sweeping the coins from the table into his hand and dropping them into his pocket. "But perhaps I won't tell her until tomorrow – I'm not sure I have the energy for her gratitude today." He winked at me again and stood, holding out his hand. "If you need any more help, Gregory, I'm your man – particularly if you're after someone to follow that French piece again."

Chapter Nineteen

COMMUNICATION

I knew the hand straight away: the note was from the Master of St Clement's. But although the script was as fine as before, this time the message was considerably more urgent. "Mr Hardiman, please come as soon as you can. I have received a worrying letter. Yours, Francis Vaughan."

Mrs Jacobs looked at me with curiosity; I rarely had anything delivered to me at my lodgings, and on a Sunday morning it was rarer still.

"Not bad news from home, I hope?" she asked.

I shook my head. "A matter in town," I said, taking my coat from the hook. "A friend in need of help."

"Will you be back for your meal?" she asked, indicating the stove. We had fallen into the habit of eating our Sunday midday meal together – she enjoyed having a hungry man to feed, and I was happy to oblige as there was little she could get wrong with roasting a piece of meat.

"I will, yes," I said, and her face brightened.

Waiting for me in that beautiful room of books, Francis Vaughan was much less composed than on my last visit. He waved the footman away impatiently and led me to a pair of seats in front of a fine desk.

"Thank you for coming so quickly, Mr Hardiman," he said. "I received a... a communication yesterday morning. I confess it disturbed my sleep, and I am not usually much troubled. But this..." He pulled a small key from his pocket and unlocked one of the desk drawers. He took out a letter and unfolded it, almost turning his face from it as he handed it to me. It was written in a neat hand on serviceable but not fine paper. The complete lack of crossings out suggested that this was a fair copy of a letter that had been carefully composed.

"Sir," I read to myself, "allow me to present myself as someone who may be able to do you a service. I am the proprietor of a small auction house in Antwerp and I was recently offered an item for sale. It is a small bronze statue of a kneeling angel, in a pose reminiscent of the Annunciation (sketch enclosed). The method of manufacture suggests a piece of some antiquity – perhaps fifteenth century – and my enquiries tell me that there is a similar statue in the collection of St Clement's College. Before I offer this piece for sale to the many collectors of such statuary, I thought you might welcome to opportunity to acquire it yourself, as a companion piece to your own, for the price of ninety guineas. If this arrangement is of interest to you, I have a man of business in England through whom we can make all necessary arrangements. I anticipate your earliest possible response. Yours, Charles McKinley, Esq. Dealer in fine art and religious statuary."

I looked up at the Master. "Ninety guineas," I said.

He nodded. "A handsome price," he said.

"For a piece you would be buying on trust," I added, "without inspecting it first. May I see the sketch?" He handed me another piece of paper with a light pencil drawing on it and I gave him the letter in exchange. "Is it like your missing statue?" I asked.

"Very like," said the Master.

"So it could simply be a companion piece," I suggested, although knowing it to be unlikely.

Vaughan shook his head. "After receiving the letter, I felt I had to take Professor Sandys into my confidence. You remember that he is a theologian?"

"Ah," I said. "And you thought he might know more than you about the statue?"

"Indeed," said the Master. "Professor Sandys was shocked and saddened, of course, to hear that other college property has gone missing. More importantly, he is of the view that statues like this – like ours – do not come in sets, with companion pieces. Although angels are frequently depicted in groups, this particular pose – as it says in the letter, reminiscent of the Annunciation – requires only the one angel. You remember your scripture, I am sure, Mr Hardiman."

I nodded. "Parts of it, at any rate," I said. "The Archangel Gabriel. And if the statue in Antwerp is unlikely to be a companion piece, you suspect it is actually your missing statue."

"I do, yes," agreed Vaughan. "The bit in the letter about Mr McKinley's enquiries sounds odd. If even our own fellows were mostly unaware of the statue's existence, how could a..." he glanced at the letter again, "a dealer in fine art and religious statuary in Antwerp find out about it?"

"I am inclined to agree with you, sir," I said, putting the sketch down on the desk.

"What should I do, Mr Hardiman?" asked the Master.

"As I see it, you have two options," I said. "You ignore the letter, and I fear that will be the last you see of your statue. McKinley – if that is indeed his name – will simply sell it. I doubt he will get the ninety guineas he asks for from you; I imagine that includes a premium he thinks you will pay to recover the piece and avoid embarrassment. But he will get something, which will give him a profit over the nothing he paid for it." The Master looked miserable and I continued. "Or you reply to the letter, telling McKinley to instruct his man of business to make himself known to you. Word your letter carefully to suggest that the whole matter must be kept secret, that no-one else knows that the piece is missing."

"Certainly, but why?" asked Vaughan.

"McKinley knows who you are," I explained. "He will assume that you are a man of books, of learning – but commercially naive. He will think that he can gull you. It helps us if he is not on his guard."

"I see," said the Master. "Very well, Mr Hardiman – I shall write the letter this afternoon."

"Please let me know as soon as you hear anything," I said, "from either McKinley or his man of business."

Chapter Twenty

THREATS

The last coach of the day, every day except Sunday, is the *Telegraph*. It starts its journey at the Golden Cross in Charing Cross and makes its way north, reaching Cambridge at about four o'clock. The driver and the horses then stay overnight at the Sun, before making the return journey at ten o'clock the next morning. For the six months or so that I had been ostler at the Sun, there had been two regular drivers on the *Telegraph* – one heading in each direction each day. Jem Reynolds is a local man, and he drives the route so that he can spend Sundays at his home on Maids' Causeway in Cambridge. The London man, driving to end his week in the capital, is John Winsome. Both are courteous and skilful, and so as soon as I saw the rear wheel of the coach clip the gate-post and heard the driver curse the horses for their clumsiness, I knew that it was neither Jem nor John at the ribbons.

I walked forward to take hold of the harness of the front horse and could tell from the rolling of its eyes and the skittish way it danced on the cobbles that it had been unnerved by its journey. The driver flung his whip to the ground and jumped down after it. All four horses backed into their traces.

"Keep hold of them, man," snarled the driver.

My concern was with the animals and so I simply ducked my head and approached the lead horse, speaking low nonsense and slowly moving my hand down its neck. I could feel its skin twitch under my touch; all four animals were wet with exertion and needed a warm stable and a good feed. One by one I unhitched them and led them into the stables, putting each into its own stall and leaving it to settle for a few minutes. Then I took up a knot of hay and rubbed down each horse, taking care to check every inch of its coat for any lumps or cuts that might need dressing before looking closely at each hoof. In this way we all five – four beasts and one man – passed a pleasant and relaxing hour. I left them dozing and went back out into the yard. The coach was now empty of passengers and luggage and young Simon was washing the dust from its wheels and doors. He looked round as I passed.

"You're to go into the bar room, Mr Hardiman, sir," he said urgently. "The driver wants to see you." He dropped his voice. "What has happened to Mr Reynolds? I don't like this new man." He rubbed his elbow as he spoke.

"What's wrong with your arm, Simon?" I asked. I stopped. "Did he hit you, the new driver?"

The lad shrugged. "I s'pose I deserved it, Mr Hardiman," he said gruffly.

"I very much doubt that, Simon," I said. "You're a good worker – Mr Reynolds always says so. You leave this new fellow to me."

Simon smiled and saluted me; someone had once told him that I was an old soldier and since then there was no convincing him that I hadn't beaten Boney single-handed.

I blinked as I walked into the inn; after the bright late afternoon sunshine outside, my eyes took a moment to adjust to the gloom inside. I walked along the corridor to the bar room where the drivers and grooms took their refreshment. It was a serviceable room, with hard chairs and yesterday's newspapers and a window giving out onto the side passage. Sitting with his back to the window, a tankard and a plate with the remains of a wedge of pie on it on the table in front of him, was the driver of the *Telegraph*. I went up to him and he leaned back in his seat, tilting his head so that he could look down his nose at me.

"Hardiman?" he asked.

I shoved my hands into my pockets; I had no wish to shake his hand.

"Hardiman," I confirmed.

"No mistaking you, is there? With all of that." He waved his hand in front of his own face. I said nothing. "I've a message for you," he said.

"Who's sending me messages through a man I don't know?" I asked.

He shook his head. "The sender's not important," he said. "But the message is." He stood up and walked around the table until he was standing next to me – too close, but I did not back away. "You're to leave well alone, Hardiman," he said. "Stop asking questions, stop sticking your nose in where it doesn't belong."

"I'm curious to find that the actions of a Cambridge ostler are of such interest to someone in London that they bother to send their slavey to warn me," I said mildly. "And I would have thought that the driver of a respected coach like the *Telegraph* would have had more dignity. Mr Reynolds would never stoop to being a messenger boy for blackguards."

The fellow blinked as though not quite believing what he was hearing. I caught a movement of his hand but just then the pot boy came into the bar room and the driver stepped away from me.

"For a farthing I'd see to you myself," he growled, "but you're not worth the trouble." He reached for his tankard and drained it. "With any luck, you'll take no notice of what I've said, and my next orders will be to finish you off." He glanced at the clock on the wall and pushed out past me, back towards the yard.

"He's a bully, that one, Mr Hardiman," said the pot boy, picking up the empty tankard.

"You know him, then?" I asked.

The pot boy shrugged. "He picks up routes here and there when other drivers are ill. Doesn't sweeten his temper, though, getting some money. I just keep clear." He went to leave the room.

"Wait," I said. "Do you know his name?"

"We all know his name – all the pot boys and yard lads in town," he said bitterly. "Hits hard and tips soft, that one. Dick Morgan. Good riddance, I say."

As I sat in my room that evening, a book open but unread in my lap, I went back over what Dick Morgan had said to me. He had been paid to deliver the warning to me, so someone in London knew that I worked at the Sun and knew that I had been asking questions – sticking my nose in, as they would have it. They were also canny enough to know when the usual driver was off and that the replacement would have no scruples about being part of their threats – or maybe, the thought occurred to me, they had supplied one of their own as the replacement driver. And they were obviously serious about halting my enquiries: the driver had hinted that if I didn't, they would kill me.

I am not one of those men who seek out danger in order to run towards it, for the thrill of it all. No-one who has seen the terror in the eyes of battlefield horses or heard the screams of a dying man begging for his mother's comfort would volunteer to look at danger again. But no more can bullies and bad men be allowed to triumph. Don't you worry: I'm not naive enough to believe the catechism promise that the meek will inherit the earth. But I do think that, with the help of good men, they can keep their foothold on it. If nothing else, the driver's warning told me that I was asking the right questions in the right places.

Chapter Twenty-One

POISON

Even the porter was quieter than usual when I knocked on the window of his lodge and told him that I was going to the Master's rooms. Word was all over town that the butler of St Clement's had killed himself. As I have said before, Cambridge is little more than a village when it comes to gossip and scandal, and I wanted to make sure of the facts before deciding what to do.

"You'll have to wait here, Mr Hardiman," said the porter, coming out of his lodge. "The Master has asked me to check with him before admitting anyone today. You can sit in the lodge, if you've a mind."

I shook my head. "I am happy to wait here," I said. "Oh," the porter turned back to me, "is Mr Lowe in college today?"

The porter nodded solemnly. "He is, yes, sir," he said, "but he's very shaken." He shook his own head sadly. "Imagine finding that. Nasty. And in the middle of term, too."

I left the porter to his thoughts. I walked along the side of the court to the dining hall and climbed the stairs to the first floor. I knocked on the door of the butler's room, and was not surprised when

Philip Lowe opened it. He looked dreadful – pale and red-eyed – and likewise not surprised to see me.

"Mr Hardiman," he said, opening the door wider. "Please come in. I was just checking the latest ledgers for orders that are due today. Forgive the smell."

The windows of the room were opened wide, but there was still a sickly smell of bitter almonds.

"They have taken the body," he said flatly. "It was there." He indicated one of the winged armchairs.

"I understand you found him, Mr Lowe," I said gently. "A terrible shock for you." He nodded wordlessly. "Here," I said, "shall we sit?" I led him to the desk and we sat down.

"It was the bloating," he said quietly. "I didn't know that happened. I thought poison was all inside." He indicated his stomach. "But his face – it was like something from a nightmare."

During one of my visits to Mr Relhan, he and I had discussed some of the poisons in his most carefully-guarded bottles. Prussic acid was an easy one for an old soldier to remember, with its name derived from the blue colour used to dye the coats for the Prussian army.

"As I understand it," I said, "most of that happens after death. He would not have felt it. Prussic acid paralyses the lungs – you stop breathing. That takes a couple of minutes and isn't pleasant – a bit like drowning – but the rest, he would have known nothing about it."

The junior butler looked at me. "The rug was all awry – I suppose he kicked out. But his face... swollen, and blue." He shook his head as though to clear it of the image.

"Try not to dwell on it, Mr Lowe," I said.

"But perhaps I could have done something, if I had found him sooner..." he said.

I shook my head. “Prussic acid works almost instantly,” I said. “The moment he swallowed it, his fate was sealed. The finest surgeon in London could not have saved him.”

“Thank you for your reassurance, Mr Hardiman,” said Lowe. “Mr Perry and I were not friends, exactly, but I have him to thank for my position here at St Clement’s, and I am sorry that he did not speak to me about his troubles.”

“What do you know of his troubles?” I asked.

Lowe looked at me and then away into the distance. He seemed to be weighing something in his mind, and eventually he put his hand into his pocket and took out a folded piece of paper. “This was in his hand when I found him,” he said. He looked down at the paper and then up at me, despairingly. “I don’t know why I took it, Mr Hardiman, really I don’t. But it sounded so private, so sad – I didn’t want strangers to read it.” He made up his mind and handed the paper to me. I unfolded it.

“I cannot go on,” I read aloud. “I have stolen from St Clement’s for many years, for my own enrichment. George Ryder has died because of my actions. I am guilty and can no longer live with that guilt. It is the end, by my own hand. Robert Perry.” I folded the paper again. “May I keep this?” I asked. “I will make sure that it reaches the right person, without mentioning how I came by it.”

Lowe nodded. "But...” he stopped.

“Is there something else, Mr Lowe?” I asked.

“It’s just that...” he started. “Hearing you read that phrase. ‘By my own hand.’ The note: I am not sure it is in Mr Perry’s own hand. I know his script well, and although it is similar, it is not the same. At first I thought that a man writing such a note might not be himself, and that might affect it, but now...” He stopped and shook his head.

“But now you are sure,” I said. “Now you are certain that Mr Perry did not write this note.” He nodded. “Then we must find who did," I said. "At the very least, they were with Mr Perry when he killed himself. And perhaps..." I left the sentence unfinished.

Back in my rooms, I took the note from my pocket and carefully flattened it on the table. I put my candle as near to it as I dared and looked closely at the script. Lowe had given me one of Perry's ledgers for comparison and I put the note onto the open ledger. I compared the formation of the letters, the space between them, and the slant of the writing. And Lowe was right: there were some similarities between the two, but they were not the same. I sat back in my chair. If Perry had not written the note, who had? And why had they done it? There was only one reason: to make a murder look like self-murder.

I looked again at the note, and something caught my eye. I turned it again to the light of the candle. And yes, there it was. I knew I had seen that distinctive miniscule *f* before. But where?

Chapter Twenty-Two

STATUE

Francis Vaughan and I took some time to decide where he should meet McKinley's man of business, Mr Frederick Boyd. It would be unwise to invite him to St Clement's, I advised, because porters have eyes everywhere, and we certainly did not want witnesses. On the other hand, it needed to be somewhere respectable, to keep up the pretence that the Master believed that there really was a reputable art dealer in Antwerp genuinely offering a piece for sale. I was also concerned for the Master's safety, although of course I did not mention that to him. If, as the warning from the coach driver and Parry's suspicious death had shown me, there was someone willing to turn to murder to protect his evil business, it was vital to be careful. In the end, I suggested that the parlour at the Hoop would serve; Vaughan could claim that he was dashing between appointments in town and had no time to return to St Clement's, and plenty of commercial meetings were held in that parlour. The arrangements were made.

Vaughan is an intelligent and well-travelled man, but he was nervous that day.

"It is not fear," he explained when I called on him just after breakfast to rehearse once more. "I am not frightened of meeting this man – after all, what can he do in the parlour at the Hoop?"

"It is simply a financial transaction," I reassured him. "Mr Boyd wants to give you a statue and walk away with ninety guineas – at any sign of trouble he will disappear, I am sure."

"Quite so," agreed the Master. "No: what troubles me is the deception." He turned to me and smiled. "I have never been any good at play-acting. When I was a child I owned up to every tiny transgression, and even as an adult I find lying all but impossible. I am concerned that this Boyd will see through me."

"Well, then," I said, "it's all a matter of how you see things. Just remind yourself that you are meeting this man to retrieve a valuable statue that rightfully belongs to St Clement's – and that is true. The other details are not important. Your purpose is true."

The Master looked at me. "Why, Mr Hardiman," he said, "I do believe you are a moral philosopher."

I laughed. "I have been called many things, Mr Vaughan," I replied, "but that's a first."

As I had hoped, the parlour at the Hoop was empty at just gone two o'clock. I had checked with the ostler and with the *Norfolk Regulator* having already departed for London there was not another coach due to leave until late in the evening. Any arrivals had already dined and set off into town on their business, and it was far too early for evening passengers to start gathering. Francis Vaughan sat in one of a pair of armchairs near the fireplace, a newspaper in his hands. I had suggested that he position himself so that he could see the door, and I was pleased to see when he glanced up as I walked past that he made no obvious sign of recognising me.

Ten minutes later I strolled past again, and now there was a man sitting with the Master. He had his back to me, but I could see that he was a slight man, with fair hair. On the floor by his chair was a battered leather bag, in which I assumed he had the statue. I signalled to the pot boy who was waiting by the kitchen door. As we had arranged, he went into the parlour to ask whether the two men required any refreshments. As he leaned between them to hear their answer, he quickly made a chalk mark on the shoulder of Boyd's coat. When he passed me in the corridor, I slipped two shillings into his hand and they immediately disappeared into the pocket of his apron.

Now all I had to do was wait. I left the Hoop and crossed the road into Dolphin Lane, keeping my eye on the entrance to the inn. After only a few minutes the slight, fair-haired man came out, carrying a leather bag, and as I walked behind him at a careful distance I could see the chalk mark on his shoulder so I was certain of my quarry. My plan was simple: to follow him to a reasonably quiet location, stop him, and explain that if he did not return the ninety guineas to me I would be taking him to the magistrate. Threatened with charges of fraud and theft, and in the shadow of the scaffold, I was sure he would make a sensible decision. As I had said to the Master, Boyd was interested simply in a commercial transaction – he was no fighter.

Boyd turned into Green Street, and I caught up with him alongside Stittle's Chapel.

"Might I have a quiet word, Mr Boyd?" I asked. I took hold of his elbow before he could object and pushed him into the yard of the meeting house.

"But who..." I heard him say, before I felt a terrible blow on the back of my head and everything went black.

"Mister! Mister!"

I opened my eyes then closed them again – the light made my head throb.

"Mister, wake up," said the voice again. "Mister, I think your friend's dead."

I swallowed hard and forced my eyes open again. Leaning over me, squatting on his haunches, was a boy of about eight, his concerned face inches from mine.

"Can you sit up?" he asked. "I can get someone if you want."

"No, no," I managed to say. "Just give me a moment." I put my hand to the back of my head and felt warm sticky blood. The boy dug into his pocket and offered me a grubby piece of cloth. "Could you go into one of the houses and see if a maid will let you dip that in some water for me?" I asked. He nodded and ran off. I put my hands to the ground behind me and managed to push myself into a sitting position. A couple of yards from me was Boyd, sprawled on his front and – as the boy had suggested – in a much worse state than I was. A pool of blood was spreading around his head. Either I had a thicker skull than he did, or our attackers had misjudged with one of us. Someone would raise the alarm soon and I had to make sure that no-one connected Boyd with St Clement's. I took a deep breath and turned my body until I was on my hands and knees, and crawled across to him. I put my fingers to his neck more as a formality than in any real hope of feeling anything – I could see clearly that he was dead. His leather bag was half trapped under his body and I pulled on the strap to free it. The statue had gone, of course – handed over to Mr Vaughan in the Hoop. But so was the money. I felt into every corner of the bag and my fingers closed on a notebook. I pulled it out; it was a small, leather-bound book, for appointments and addresses and the like. I slipped it into my pocket just as the boy returned with the damp cloth and two men from the bookbinders up the road.

I was thankful that Mrs Jacobs was out when I arrived home. Her care and ministrations would have been welcome, but her inevitable questions would not. I filled my water jug and took it up to my room, and carefully rinsed my head over the basin. The men from the bookbinders had assured me that the cut was small, but head wounds bleed like the Devil. I created a clean pad from two handkerchiefs and positioned it over the cut with one hand while using the other to wind a scarf around my head to keep the pad in place. I shook a tablet from my brown bottle and carefully broke it in half; I knew enough from the battlefield not to go to sleep with a bleeding head, but I needed to relax. I was shivering and so I sat in my armchair, tucking a blanket around my knees like a grandmother at her fireside. I reached across to my coat hanging on the hook and pulled out Boyd's notebook from the pocket.

I turned to the last page with anything written on it, about a third of the way through the book, and there was a note of his appointment with Francis Vaughan: "Vaughan, 2 o'c, Hoop, Cam". Earlier pages showed similar notes, although nothing in Cambridge – most were in London and the surrounding counties. I turned then to the front of the notebook and saw a name on the flyleaf: "Property of James Horwood, November 1824". Frederick Boyd had been a false name – a precaution against discovery. But Horwood was a name I knew well. And suddenly, blindingly, everything pointed in one direction.

Chapter Twenty-Three

PEGLEG

I was eating my midday snack in the loft above the stables when I heard a tread on the ladder and the head of Simon the yard lad appeared.

"Sorry to disturb you, Mr Hardiman, sir," he said, "but there's a gentleman here to see you. I said he should go to the parlour and you would come to him, but he's here. Wants to come up."

"Send him up, then, Simon," I said.

Simon's head disappeared down below and then popped up again.

"He'll be slow on the ladder, sir," he whispered. "He's a pegleg."

Simon climbed down again and a few moments later the ladder opening was filled by the substantially larger frame of Mr John Galpin, Bursar of St Clement's. He reached for the banister and hauled himself up, waving away my offer to help.

"Thanks to Mr Potts," said the Bursar, ducking his head and clumping over to the armchair I indicated, "it can do almost everything my other leg can manage – except tiptoe quietly about the place." He turned and dropped into the chair, removing his hat and putting it onto the floor beside him. I could see now that he was a handsome man, his silvering hair swept back from what would once have been called a noble brow.

"Mr Potts?" I asked.

"The fellow who invented this," said Galpin, tapping on his wooden leg. "Or at least, made it more useful, so that it bends at the knee and the ankle. Useful for a cripple like me, and a Godsend for so many old soldiers. I see that you have your own cross to bear." He indicated the side of his face. "Where were you?" Something about his genuine interest made me decide to tell him.

"I joined up when I was fifteen," I said, "and was put to work with the horses – horses seem to like me." As if it had heard me, a horse in the stables below us gave a loud neigh, and Galpin smiled delightedly. "I was with the 48th Northamptonshire. We went to Gibraltar and on to Spain, and by then I was servant to an officer. A good man, and I was happy to work for him. Then we fought at Albuera, in '11." I paused. "You read of it?"

The Bursar nodded. "A bloody business, by all accounts. And that's where...?" He indicated his face again.

"Yes," I said. And in the quiet of that loft above a Cambridge coaching inn I could somehow hear the roars and the screams, smell the gunpowder and the sweat and the blood and the terror. I thought of the little brown bottle waiting for me in my coat pocket, but I resisted. "I was behind the battlefield when I received word that Major Howard's charger had been killed and that I was to take his second horse up to him. It was like walking into Hell." I stopped to gather my thoughts. Galpin sat silently. I continued. "I reached the major – he was shaken, but uninjured. Prince – his horse – had been shot from beneath him; thank God a clean shot through the head so the animal did not suffer. I helped Major Howard to mount and just at that moment the call went up to form square. The major shouted at me to run back, but it was too late. I turned and pushed and shoved and scrambled as best I could, but with officers charging and the French lancers all but upon them... I was lucky to escape with just this. A sabre, they told me – one of our own or a Frenchie's, who can say. I stumbled to the dressing station and they patched me up with sticking plaster – it did the job, but it's not pretty."

"It's no elegant duelling scar, that's true," said the Bursar, "but it's more honest."

I shrugged. "If war is honest," I replied.

"Ah, well," said Galpin, raising an eyebrow, "that is a question for the philosophers, not a mere chemist."

"Nor an ostler," I agreed. "And indeed, I am wondering quite what you think this ostler can do for you, Mr Galpin."

"Ah, so you do know who I am," he said. "I wondered when we met that day in Sidney Street."

"Much as I am known for this," I pointed at my cheek, "you are known for that." And I indicated his leg. I was certainly not going to admit that I had been following him that day – let him think it was a chance encounter.

"And you know my college," he continued. I nodded. "You have been talking to people there about missing items – food, wine and so on." I had not hidden my visits to St Clement's and I was not surprised that word of them had reached the Bursar's ears. I nodded again. "And you doubtless wonder why I have not done a better job of managing the college finances."

"As I understand it," I said, "the practical management of the college finances is in the hands of the butler, not the Bursar. In ordinary times."

"When the butler has not killed himself, you mean," said Galpin. I must have looked shocked. "Forgive me: that was unkind. And, I fear, untrue." He looked at me searchingly.

"Untrue?" I repeated.

"Mr Hardiman, you know that I am a chemist," said the Bursar, leaning forward in his seat. "A practical man, dealing with the organic compounds that make life possible. Life, and death. Mr

Perry, God rest his soul, died from ingesting Prussic acid – which everyone knows is popular with those bent on self-murder, thanks to its quick-acting nature. But there are two things that concern me. Firstly, there was no note found with the body, and most self-murderers like to explain themselves. And secondly, Mr Perry was a vain man."

I frowned. "A vain man? What does that signify?"

"Poisoning by Prussic acid is an ugly way to die," explained Galpin. "The bloating, the dark discolouration of the skin, the foul smell. Mr Perry would not have chosen that. There are other less... disturbing poisons to choose. Cyanide, for example. Or arsenic. Both easy to come by, both quick in their result if ingested in large enough quantities, both less outwardly disfiguring than Prussic acid." He laughed. "You look quite horrified, Mr Hardiman. No doubt you thought we chemists were dusty academics, like the theologians and mathematicians. But no, we laboratory men like to get our hands dirty." He held them up as illustration, and indeed there were stains on several of the fingers.

"If you do not think it was self-murder..." I started.

Galpin sat back in his chair. "Yes, I think it was murder. Murder made – rather clumsily made, but there you go – to look like self-murder."

"And you have told the coroner of your concerns?" I asked.

The Bursar looked a little uneasy. "I will of course tell him," he said, "but I wanted to see you first."

"Me?" I said. "Why on earth would you think to see me about this?"

"Mr Hardiman, we have already established that you have been looking into the financial misdoings at St Clement's. And I am sure that you know of Mr Perry's," he searched for the right word, "unwise dealings with certain suppliers to the college." He looked at me for confirmation.

"I know of suspicions about Mr Perry's dealings with certain suppliers," I allowed.

"And, to be frank, Mr Hardiman," said Galpin firmly, "I would like you to tell me if you have found out anything that can identify those involved. The matter has become quite urgent – quite urgent for me personally."

"Beyond your desire to see Mr Perry's attacker – if there is one – brought to justice, I do not see how this concerns you so personally," I said. "Or why you have not simply gone to the authorities." I waited.

The Bursar hesitated. He gnawed at the edge of a fingernail, then looked at me again, as though sizing me up. Finally he reached into his coat pocket and took out a folded piece of paper. "I found this," he said, "left this morning for me. Put into this very pocket when my coat was hanging on a hook in the office next to my laboratory. My private office." He looked at the paper and then handed it to me.

I unfolded it and read it. "Perry changed his mind and you see what happened to him. Do not make the same mistake or it will go badly for you." It was, of course, unsigned. But the miniscule *f* was familiar.

Chapter Twenty-Four

LEDGER

Geoffrey Giles was waiting for me behind the counter of Nicholson's. I had sent word the day before that I would be grateful for a few minutes of his time, and that if at all possible he should have to hand the minutes from the book club. It was extremely fortunate for me that he is currently the president and as such has ready access to the club's ledgers.

The bookseller raised his hand in welcome and then pointed to the back of the shop. I nodded and we went through the heavy curtain into the parlour. He offered me a drink but I declined.

"I am very sorry to make such a request of you, Mr Giles," I said straight away.

"I am intrigued," he replied. "I cannot imagine what there may be of interest in the minutes of our rather dull little club, but I know that you would not ask unless it were important." He retrieved a leather satchel from a hook where it was hanging and took from it a ledger that I recognised from our meetings at the Black Bull Inn. He looked at it for a moment and then handed it to me. We both sat down in the sagging armchairs.

I opened the book to the most recent page and then turned back. "So you became president on the first of April?" I asked.

"If that was a Wednesday," said Giles. "If not, it was on the first Wednesday of the month."

"Here it is," I said, finding the minutes of that meeting. "Wednesday the sixth of April 1825."

"There you are," agreed the bookseller.

"And before your term, the president was Mr Horwood – Robert Horwood," I said.

"Indeed," said Giles, nodding. "He was the president when you joined us, I recall."

"And so," I said, turning back a few more pages of the ledger, "this would be his hand here?" I turned the ledger so that the bookseller could see it. "These minutes here?"

Giles nodded. "Yes: you can see his signature at the end of the page, there." He pointed. "Why does this interest you? It will be a little while before you are called on to serve as president; you will be a librarian first and then the steward. But if you are uneasy about the responsibility..." He stopped as I shook my head.

"I cannot tell you why just yet," I explained, "but what interests me is not the minutes but rather the hand in which they are written. Mr Horwood's hand. I know it is a great deal to ask when I can tell you so little, but would you permit me to borrow this ledger for a few hours?"

"As long as you return it to me in time for our meeting on Wednesday," said Giles, "I have no objection."

In one of those odd coincidences we all experience occasionally, I was walking back along Trinity Street towards the Sun when I saw Robert Horwood step out of the Blue Boar. We caught sight of each other at the same moment; I tucked the ledger tighter under my arm, while – if I was not mistaken – he made a quick signal to someone behind him. I drew level with him.

"Mr Hardiman," he said with great warmth, holding out his hand, which I shook. "You are returning to the Sun?"

"I am indeed, Mr Horwood," I said. "There are two coaches to see to at half-past noon, and I have yet to feed the horses."

"Are you happy working at the Sun?" he asked.

"It is a good establishment," I said. "Mr Bird allows me enough time and money to make sure that the animals are well-treated."

"It may seem an impertinent question," said Horwood, dropping his voice, putting his hand on my elbow and guiding me away from the door of the inn. "But I hear whispers that Mr Bird may be moving from this street to one just behind." He jerked his head to indicate. "From one circular establishment to another, you might say."

"To Bridge Street?" I asked. "You mean the Hoop?"

"That's what I hear," said Horwood, still walking with his hand on my elbow, and turning with me into Dolphin Lane. Just then the clock of All Saints-in-the-Jewry chimed the hour. "Goodness me, is it eleven already?" said my companion. "You will forgive me if I leave you." And he darted off into Trinity Street again.

I turned back towards the corner myself and carefully peeped around it. As Horwood reached the doorway of the Blue Boar once more, he held out his hand and a woman took hold of it and stepped out into the street. She was in an elegant dark grey frock, her rich chestnut hair gathered in a neat bun at her neck. Horwood tucked her hand into the crook of his arm and the two of them walked away from me, leaning their heads towards each other. I heard her laughing. For a man in mourning, he was in surprisingly good spirits.

Chapter Twenty-Five

CHESTERTON

I was checking the hay store to make sure that none of it was going dusty and had just set a trap for the rat that one of the maids had seen that morning when Simon the lad appeared in the stables.

"There's a message for you, Mr Hardiman," he said, holding out a note. "Can I take an answer for you?" His eyes shone at the thought of earning a coin from the errand.

I straightened up and stretched my back, and took the note from him. "If it needs an answer, Simon," I said, "you'll be the very man for the job." I unfolded the paper and read it, then looked at Simon. "Right: you're to go to Mr Ryder the fishmonger, on the market, and tell him to call on me here at three o'clock. Can you remember that?" I dug into my coat pocket.

Simon nodded eagerly and repeated the message perfectly, taking the coin from me and smiling broadly at it before haring out of the yard.

At a couple of minutes past three o'clock the fishmonger knocked on the door of the stables, where I was checking the hoof of an animal that had seemed unwilling to stand on it.

"Good of you to see me, Mr Hardiman," he said, a sight more polite than at our last meeting.

"Mr Ryder," I said, straightening the horse's leg and patting it reassuringly on the shoulder. "It is too warm to sit in the loft today, so shall we take a short stroll?"

I stuck my head into the kitchen to tell them that I was going out but would be back in plenty of time for the Bury departure, and then the fishmonger and I walked out onto Trinity Street and turned our step away from town.

"I assume you wanted to see me about Mr Perry?" I asked.

Ryder glanced quickly at me and then away. "Aye," he said. "Killed himself."

"So they say," I replied. "We shall see."

"What do you mean?" asked the fishmonger.

"When we last met," I continued, ignoring his question, "you told me you knew that Mr Perry had been lining his own pockets at the expense of his college. And something similar was mentioned in a note found in his room." As I had promised Mr Lowe, I had made sure that the note he had found had been passed anonymously to the coroner.

"Ha!" said Ryder. He seemed pleased with himself.

"The accuracy of your information," I said, "makes me wonder whether you knew more about Mr Perry than you told me last time."

Ryder stopped. His weaselly face looked less pleased now. "More?" he asked. "What do you mean?"

"Well," I said, lowering my voice and beckoning him close, "it appears that Mr Perry was not the only one in that college lining his own pocket."

The fishmonger's face crinkled with pleasure. "I thought as much," he said smugly. "There's not much you can keep secret in one of them colleges."

"Indeed, Mr Ryder," I said confidingly. "I have been hearing all sorts of stories. Even some involving Mr Galpin – the Bursar."

Ryder nodded emphatically. "That's what I'd heard too." He leaned even closer, which was not altogether pleasant given his profession. "One of the kitchen lads told me he'd seen Mr Perry and Mr Galpin arguing, and that Mr Galpin handed Mr Perry something – some money, he thought."

"Payment for some supplies, perhaps," I suggested.

"He'd do that out in the open," objected the fishmonger. "Sounds more like blackmail to me."

"And you would know, Mr Ryder," I almost said out loud, but I caught myself. "Interesting," I said instead.

"Isn't it," agreed Ryder.

We walked on. "But tell me, Mr Ryder," I said after a few moments. "Why did you ask to see me today?"

He stopped again. "Mr Hardiman," he said. "Now that Mr Perry is dead, God rest his soul," and he crossed himself and bowed his head in a great show of piety, "and he has confessed to what he did, I was wondering if we could keep my name out of it. With the University."

"How so?" I asked.

"You know how they work," he said urgently. "If word gets out about, well, any of it, you know what they can do."

"Discommuning, you mean?" I asked.

He nodded. "If they decide against me, I can say farewell to all the college business, and if an undergraduate so much as buys a herring from me, he'll be fined. It would be the end of me, Mr Hardiman."

"Indeed it would," I agreed. All the tradesmen in Cambridge lived in fear of discommuning, although it was thankfully rare. And in all honesty if the Chancellor decided that Ryder was untrustworthy there was nothing I would be able to do about it. But Ryder seemed to think I had great influence, and that was my good fortune. "I will do what I can," I said, choosing my words carefully, "if you will do something for me in return."

Ryder's face turned hard again, but he had little choice and he knew it. "Go on, then," he said.

"Last month I had an interesting discussion with a coach driver," I said. "He warned me to stop asking questions or things would go badly for me. I need to know who sent him."

"How am I supposed to know that?" asked the fishmonger.

"You might or you might not," I conceded, "but you can at least ask around. The market is full of suppliers and visitors from London – one of them might know something."

Ryder shrugged. "I can try," he agreed, "if you'll try to help me with the University." I nodded. "Then what's the driver's name?" he asked.

"Dick Morgan," I said. "A bit taller than me, lean, very dark hair, long nose."

"Dick Morgan," repeated the fishmonger slowly. "It's a common enough name, and it may be something and nothing, but I do know of a Dick Morgan related to the Greenway brothers. A cousin from out Ely way."

After supper that evening, I told Mrs Jacobs that I was going out for a stroll to clear my head. And indeed it was a pleasure to walk across Butts Green towards the sluice, take the ferry across the river, and then walk along the edge of Chesterton Fen. The trees lining the river were in full leaf, providing room and board for all manner of birds who called and whistled as I passed. I cut up across the field past the manor house, along Church Lane and into the High Street. It was a while since I had visited Chesterton, and I could see several new premises in this thriving village.

The Maltster's Arms was a substantial property, with the public house facing onto the street and a large malthouse and kiln in the back yard. It was this yard that provided the entertainment for which the place was so popular: pugilism. When I was a lad, prize fighting was a respectable way to earn a living. Indeed, I could remember officers betting large amounts on the outcome when news reached us in Spain that the English champion Tom Crib would be fighting the American challenger Tom Molineaux in, I think, late '11. But now, in these more enlightened times, the spectacle of two men beating each other for public entertainment is no longer tolerated as part of polite society, and those who wish to see it – and there are plenty who still do – have to make their way to places like this. And it was the keeper of the public house, Isaac Platten, I wanted to see.

I had known of Zack Platten for as long as I could remember. Like me he was a Norfolk man, and when I was no more than five, my father had taken me to see Zack in a prize fight. My brother was too young and there was no question of my sister coming, and I was pleased as Punch to be out on an adventure with just my father. We walked for more than three hours to see the spectacle, held in a field outside Norwich. There was a roped-off square in the middle of the grass, and hundreds of people crowded around, pushing and elbowing to get to the front. My father hoisted me onto his shoulders and I had the best view of all. Waiting around the edge of the field were dozens of barouches, landaus and even phaetons, which fascinated me just as much as the fight we had come to see. And when the fight started, the aristocratic young men who had arrived in those fine carriages yelled and shouted just as vigorously as those of us who had travelled by Shanks' pony.

Zack Platten was in his prime then; about twenty years old, he was as strong as a bull, with the broad shoulders and thick thighs that come from heavy work on the land. Moreover, he was a local lad, and we cheered ourselves hoarse whenever he landed a blow on his opponent – a skinnier fellow from somewhere up north. It took only six rounds for Zack to claim victory, but my father pointed out how the victor took care to help his defeated opponent from the ring. "The mark of a gentleman, that is, Gregory," I remember him saying. "Grace in victory and defeat."

And life had knocked none of that kindness out of Zack. As I walked into the bar room, he reversed out of the kitchen, two tankards in each large hand, and as he turned and caught sight of me, his face broke into a wide smile.

"Gregory Hardiman!" he boomed. "Let me just..." he deposited the tankards on a table, where they were seized thirstily by four men, and then came over to me. He took hold of my hand – always a dangerous moment when dealing with a pugilist – and shook it energetically, meanwhile clapping me on the shoulder. "Have a seat, have a seat," he said, waving to the pot boy and holding up two fingers. I did as I was told, two tankards appeared on the table in front of us, and Zack and I raised them to each other's health. "'Tis a great pleasure to see you, young Gregory," he said, wiping his mouth with the back of his hand.

I laughed. "Not so young any more, Zack," I said, shaking my head.

"Young compared to this square toes," replied the keeper. To be sure, his face showed his age and his former profession, with a nose more broken than whole, but his grip was fierce and he still resembled a barrel on legs. "Now, with you working at an inn yourself," he continued, "I know you've not come all this way for a tankard and a mardle. So how can old Zack help you?"

I told him what had happened in the past few weeks and he listened carefully. "And I had assumed that the driver had been paid by someone in London, concerned in the valuable thefts from the college," I finished, "but it turns out that he is just a country cousin of the Greenway brothers who thinks he's a city bruiser. And it's all to do with protecting the grubby trade they have with college kitchens."

"The Greenway brothers," said Zack grimly, "are nothing but trouble."

"You've had quarrels with them?" I asked.

"Not personally, no," he replied. "They rarely leave the town, those boys. But I know of them."

"Well, that's all the better as far as I am concerned," I said, and I laid out my plan.

Chapter Twenty-Six

SHADOWS

Being so close to Slaughterhouse Lane and Butcher Row the air in Sparrow Lane was never very fresh, but on this still, warm evening it was truly eye-watering. I took a moment to steel myself and then nodded to the three men with me as we walked into the gloom of the narrow street. The untidy buildings leaned in towards each other and the cobbles, even after the heat of the day, were slick with God knows what. In one doorway a naked toddler squatted, digging between the stones with a stick, while in another a girl of about twelve looked at us with mild curiosity before turning to answer some call from inside her home. At a third, an old man sat on an upturned wooden crate, biting the end of his pipe and watching the world go by.

According to my information, the Greenway brothers lived in the last house but one, with their parents and younger sister. Jem Greenway's woman also lived there; she called herself Mrs Green-way but few believed they had troubled the church with their union. The door was closed. My two companions held back as I knocked on it. It was opened by the taller of the brothers.

I nodded at him. "You'll remember me," I said. "Hardiman, from the Sun. I'd like a word with you and your brother."

He shut the door in my face and I could hear him calling. A few moments later Jem appeared.

"Mr Greenway," I said pleasantly. "I wanted to give you a message to pass on, to your cousin Mr Morgan."

Jem Greenway's face darkened. His brother loomed up behind him.

"You don't learn your lesson, do you, Mr Hardiman," growled Jem. "Now, we've tried to be polite. We had a quiet word with you back in, what was it Sam, February?"

"Yes, Jem – February," agreed his brother.

"And then when you took no notice we had Dick make it even clearer to you, didn't we, Sam?"

"Yes, Jem – even clearer," echoed his brother.

"And yet still," said Jem, making a fist and rubbing its knuckles with his other hand, "and yet still you seem to need convincing. So let's see to that now, shall we?" He stood to one side and Sam stepped out into the street. "We're just going out, Mother," Jem called back into the house before shutting the door behind him.

"I'm glad I find you with the time to spare, Mr Greenway," I said smoothly, "as my friends are busy men."

As I said this, Zack Platten and the two lads he had brought with him stepped out of the shadows. I had asked Zack to find two men who would not be afraid of a bit of milling, and he had certainly done that. The pair were due to appear in the yard of the Maltster's Arms this very evening, and their toughness was obvious in their stance and in the scars on their faces and hands. I heard a scraping as doors all along Sparrow Lane were hastily closed, their inhabitants disappearing inside.

"Well, now, Mr Hardiman," said Jem Greenway, "I am sure there's no need for this."

"We were hoping you'd see it our way, weren't we, boys?" said Zack. The two brawny lads flanking him nodded, although I could see disappointment on both their faces. I think they had looked forward to an opportunity to practise their craft. "Now, Mr Greenway, I think Mr Hardiman has a few suggestions as to how you and he can come to a friendly understanding."

Jem folded his arms but said nothing.

"Now, as I recall you telling me back in February," I began, "you two are responsible for the death of George Ryder." Jem opened his mouth to speak but I held up a hand and Zack made to move forward. Jem shut his mouth. "I understand that you didn't mean to kill him," I continued, "but nevertheless you did kill him. And left his wife and family without his wage. Now, there is nothing you can do for Mrs Ryder to make up for the man she has lost, but you can make up for the wage." I waited. "You can pay her, Mr Greenway."

He shuffled on the spot. "I suppose we could give her a little something each week..." he started.

I shook my head. "The last thing Mrs Ryder needs is to be reminded each and every week of what you have done. This is what will happen. You will make her a single payment of thirty pounds now, and then each month you will deliver five pounds to me. That's what her husband would have brought home, and I will make sure it reaches her. You will continue these monthly payments until either her youngest child starts earning his own wage, or Mrs Ryder marries again. Is that clear?"

"Thirty pounds," repeated Jem. "That's a tidy sum."

"I'm not a heartless man," I said. "I'll give you a month to find it."

Chapter Twenty-Seven

Vanilla

Now that I knew for certain that the Greenways were behind the death of George Ryder, I had something to tell the Master of St Clement's. The porter was sitting on a stool outside his lodge, fanning himself with a newspaper.

"Warm enough for you, Mr Hardiman?" he asked. "It's a blessing to be so sheltered in winter," he indicated the high walls of the college, "but in the summer I would give my eye-teeth for a fresh breeze."

"I'm not as bothered by the heat as I once was," I replied. "I think my blood must have thinned after so many years in Spain and Australia – now that was hot."

The porter's eyebrows raised. "You've been to New Holland?" he asked.

I nodded. "When I was in the army, yes."

"I hear it is full of cannibals and convicts," said the porter, his eyes shining.

I laughed. "Convicts, yes, but no cannibals – or at least, none that we know of. But it's a harsh land and no mistake."

The porter shuddered. "Not for me, Mr Hardiman. Cambridge born and bred, me, and if I get my way, I'll die here too."

"Not too soon, I hope, Mr..." I replied.

"Chapman," he said. "George Chapman." He held out his hand and I shook it.

"Is the Master in his rooms, Mr Chapman?" I asked.

"He is, yes – would you like me to take you up?" He made a reluctant move to rise from his stool.

I shook my head. "I know the way, Mr Chapman."

I found the Master struggling to open one of his windows.

"Ah, Mr Hardiman," he said, smiling. "Just the man. Here: if I push this lower corner while holding the stay out of the way, could you just step up onto that stool and push gently at the top corner? These old windows may be picturesque," he grunted as we both pushed, "but the hinges are stiff and if you put too much strain on one corner you can bend the frame. Ah – there it goes. Goodness, that feels better already." He leaned on the sill and breathed deeply. "Still warm, but at least there is something of a breeze. Thank you, Mr Hardiman."

I stepped down off the stool and shook his hand.

"Now, timely though your visit is to save me from suffocating in this heat," said Mr Vaughan, "I assume that was not your purpose in calling on me."

"Indeed not, sir, no," I said.

"Then you have some news for me?" he asked.

I nodded. "About the activities of Mr Perry," I said.

"Ah," said the Master. "Poor Mr Perry." He shook his head. "But first, a glass of barley water?"

"That would be most welcome," I said. The Master filled two tumblers from the jug standing on the side table and handed one to me. He lifted a chair and placed it in front of the newly-opened window and then carried over a second one. We sat.

"Well," I began. "You remember my mentioning the Greenway brothers to you?" Vaughan nodded. "My suspicions about them were right: they were behind the kitchen and cellar thefts here at St Clement's – and indeed at other colleges. You were not singled out."

"There is cold comfort in that," said the Master ruefully. "It simply tells us that the butlers of several colleges are corruptible."

"Having had dealings with them," I said, "I don't think we should be too harsh on anyone who gives in to the demands of the Greenway brothers. I had to resort to heavy-handed tactics myself." And I told him about Zack Platten.

Vaughan listened quietly until I had finished. "They sound like very unpleasant men," he said at the end. "It would certainly explain why Mr Perry could no longer tolerate the Greenways constantly threatening him. Poor man." He shook his head.

I made up my mind. "Mr Vaughan," I said, "I have been undecided about telling you this, but as I am going to need you to go to the coroner with new information about Mr Perry, I can see no other way forward."

"New information about Mr Perry?" asked the Master. "Concerning what?"

"His state of mind," I replied. "Whether he was the sort of man who would kill himself."

The Master looked at me sharply. "You have reason to believe that it was not self-murder?"

I told him about the letter that Mr Lowe had found, and that it had not been written by Mr Perry. I did not mention that I thought I knew who had written it.

Vaughan sat back in his chair and breathed out. "Well," he said. "This puts a very different complexion on the matter. If the Greenways are so keen to protect their profit that they will resort to murder..."

I held up a hand. "I am no friend of the Greenways, Mr Vaughan, but I am not at all sure that I see their hand in this."

"But they killed that man, the cook from the inn," protested the Master.

"George Ryder," I said. "Yes, but that was negligence – an accident rather than deliberate murder. Manslaughter, that's the word." I held up both hands. "Or at least, I think that's what will be found once the coroner has all the evidence. They are thugs, the Greenways, thugs and bullies, but they are not assassins."

"Assassins!" repeated Vaughan. "That's quite the accusation." He stood and went to the window again, then turned to face me. "But if it was not the Greenways, who do you think did kill Mr Perry? And why?"

I shook my head. "I am only a step or two ahead of you, Master," I confessed. "I have ideas, but that is all they are. We need more information." I stood. "Would you be willing to come with me to call on the Bursar?" I asked.

Vaughan and I walked down the staircase into the court, then up another staircase. There was a sturdy wooden door with BURSAR written on it in gold script, and the Master knocked loudly.

"Mr Galpin," he called. "Mr Galpin, it is Mr Vaughan, with Mr Hardiman. Are you within?" He knocked again. There was no answering call. The Master pushed the door open and walked into the Bursar's rooms; I followed him.

The Bursar was clearly not a man who embraced order. There were books spilling off shelves onto the floor, papers tumbling from the desk, curtains half-opened.

The Master turned to me and must have seen the surprise on my face. "Do not be alarmed, Mr Hardiman," he said with some amusement. “There has not been a burglary. Mr Galpin is like many studious men: he lives so much in his mind that he fails to notice the corporeal chaos around him.” He stooped to pick up a cushion from the floor and plumped it, intending to put it on a nearby chair. We looked at each other.

“Did you smell that?” I asked.

The Master nodded and put the cushion to his own nose and then held it out to mine.

“Perfume,” I said.

“Recent perfume,” said Vaughan. “Women’s perfume.”

“Is Mr Galpin a widower?” I asked. “Does he have a daughter who visits him, or a sister?”

The Master shook his head, sniffing the cushion again. “The Bursar is a bachelor,” he said. “And an only child, I believe.” He frowned slightly. “This scent is familiar... Ah, yes, vanilla.”

He passed the cushion to me and I inhaled. “Vanilla,” I agreed. “Not a scent that many women wear... or at least, not in England.” An image flashed into my mind of Lucia and a stroll in the cooling shade of an evening garden. I put the cushion onto a chair.

“So Mr John Galpin is not the dry chemist we had imagined,” said the Master jovially. “Instead, he entertains exotic, scent-wearing ladies in his rooms, somehow spiriting them past the curious eye of Mr Chapman. But he is not here now, so we shall have to delay our questioning.” He held out his arm to shepherd me towards the door. When we reached the foot of the staircase the Master shook my hand and turned to go back to his own rooms. Partway across the court he stopped. “Mr Hardiman,” he called. “If you hear of Mr Platten putting on another spectacle, please do let me know. There’s nothing quite as exhilarating to watch as a prize fight.”

CHAPTER TWENTY-EIGHT

FAMILY

As the sun was shining that Saturday afternoon in early June, I decided to make a pleasant stroll of my errand. I took a route past Christ's Pieces and Parker's Piece, both busy with courting couples and shrieking children, before I turned into Lensfield Road. Developers had realised that there were plenty in Cambridge who would pay for a modern villa in this healthy location, and the builders were plainly still hard at work, judging by the piles of equipment and supplies. I headed for one of the new villas and admired its neat lines and large windows as I walked up the front steps.

A silent, large-eyed maid, whose eyes grew even wider when she saw my face, showed me into the front room, dropping a hasty curtsy as she stole another look at me. The room had a high ceiling with an elaborate rose at the centre, and light poured in through the tall windows. I liked to feel such openness while indoors. I was smiling to myself when the door opened and my host came in.

George Howard was in his early sixties but looked older. When I had first met him he had been much more vigorous. Major Howard had hidden the severity of his illness from his parents, writing only that he was in need of rest, but when we finally arrived in Cambridge after that endless, desperate journey there was no more hiding. He was a beloved youngest son and his painful and grisly death had broken the spirit of both parents. His father had aged seemingly overnight, his hair greying and his back stooping until he resembled a man a decade older. His mother had taken to her bed and now lived the shadowed life of an invalid. My heart grieves for both of them, as I am sure does yours.

"Mr Hardiman," said Mr Howard warmly, shaking my hand in both of his. "How kind of you to answer my invitation, fearful dull company that we are. You are well, I trust?"

"I am, sir, thank you," I replied.

"Please, please," said my host, indicating a sofa. On the low table in front of it was set a tray with a coffee pot, two cups and a plate of dainty biscuits under a white cloth. We both sat. Mr Howard lifted the coffee pot – it seemed something of an effort – and carefully poured two cups. He handed one to me. "Do have as many biscuits as you can," he said. "The cook does everything she can to tempt me, but I have little appetite these days." And indeed, his coat and trousers hung loose on his spare frame.

The coffee was delicious, as were the biscuits, and I said so. Mr Howard smiled with pleasure.

"And how is life at the Sun?" he asked. "You are comfortable?"

I nodded. "Mr Bird is a good master," I said, "and my rooms in Jesus Lane are clean and quiet. Although my landlady could use a few cooking lessons from your kitchen." I took another biscuit.

"They were William's favourite," said Mr Howard, his eyes damp. We were both silent for a moment.

"I was admiring the ceiling," I said, pointing. "The rose."

Mr Howard recollected himself. "Yes: fine workmanship. It is a very... elegant house." He smiled wanly. "I had hoped, Mr Hardiman, that a change of location would help us – that leaving behind the family home where William..." He stopped and shook his head. "But it turns out that he lives here." He put his hand on his heart.

Then he reached into a pocket for his handkerchief and dabbed at his eyes. "Forgive me: I am a foolish old man."

I shook my head. "You are a loving father, and there is nothing to forgive in that."

"You are too kind, Mr Hardiman," said my host. "But now, to business. I did not ask you here eat to biscuits and reminisce. No: it is the future I wish to discuss."

"The future?" I asked.

"Well, your future, to be precise," he replied. He sat a little more upright. "Now, as William may have mentioned to you, I have connections with the University. I was a scholar, oh, centuries ago now, and I am occasionally asked to offer my legal advice on matters of property. They say that I can provide something of a worldly view, having sampled life outside the college walls."

"A valuable view, I am sure," I said.

Mr Howard shrugged. "Perhaps," he allowed. "I am glad to be asked and happy to do what I can. Tell me, Mr Hardiman: have you heard of the University Proctors?"

I thought for a moment. "I have heard the term, yes," I replied, "but do not ask me exactly what a Proctor does." I took out my vocabulary book in readiness.

Howard watched me write in it. "An excellent idea," he said. "O R at the end, not E R." I corrected the word and he continued. "Each year two Proctors are appointed by the University. To ensure fairness, they are taken from each college in turn. In centuries gone by, the Proctors performed all sorts of ceremonial duties. But nowadays, the two of them spend a good deal of time chasing undergraduates around the streets, collaring them when they misbehave, and making sure they are back in college before the gates are locked. Or at least, they try – but some of the Proctors are even more ancient than I am. And the recent ban on horse-racing for undergraduates has added to their responsibilities. In short, they are no longer up to the job. A few years ago their ranks were swelled by the appointment of two Pro-Proctors – but they are hardly more nimble, and the colleges are complaining that their scholars are running wild. You have doubtless seen some of it yourself, around town and at the Sun." I nodded and Howard continued. "Parliament is soon to pass a law to allow the university authorities of Cambridge and Oxford to appoint some men to assist the Proctors in rounding up the miscreants. These men are to be called university constables. And – if you will permit me, Mr Hardiman – I would like to recommend you for the position."

"Me, Mr Howard?" I asked, genuinely surprised. "But I know nothing of undergraduates and what to do with them."

"The role of the constable is to be, I am told, quite a physical one," explained my host. "Each Proctor or Pro-Proctor on his patrol around town will be accompanied by two constables. The plan is to pair the constables carefully: one sprinter and one distance runner." He smiled mischievously. "If a misbehaving undergraduate is spotted, the sprinter will try to nab him. If the quarry escapes, the distance man will take over and run him to ground."

"Ah, so Major Howard told you of my youthful exploits," I said. "Running to Norwich and back for a wager."

"Ten miles, apparently," said Howard.

"Twelve," I corrected him, smiling. "But I already have employment, Mr Howard. I enjoy being an ostler."

"Ah, but that's the beauty of it," said my host, looking pleased. "The university constables will be needed only in the evening, from about six o'clock to ten o'clock. And not every evening: the University hopes to recruit a dozen constables and only four will be on duty each night. So I am sure you could make it fit with your duties at the inn. And there'd be the salary too – not a great amount, but a few pounds would come in handy, I'm sure."

"Well, it's certainly something to consider," I said. He was right: a few extra pounds would make all the difference in Spain. Before too long my daughter would be thinking of her dowry.

"I have already sung your praises to Henry Venn – he's at Queen's, and one of the current Proctors," added Howard. "And if you do decide to go ahead, I'm certain you'd be appointed."

"It is very kind of you to go to this trouble for me, Mr Howard," I said. I paused, choosing my words. "I meant what I said, you know – when Major Howard was so ill. You need never fear that I would ever say anything about... the nature of his illness."

"My wife spoke in haste that day," said Howard. "She was not herself. Not for one moment did she – did either of us – really think that you would. She was wrong to suggest otherwise, and bitterly regrets it."

"I am sorry to hear that," I said. "Please tell her that there is no need for regret; she was naturally concerned for her son's reputation and did not know me from Adam. Mr Howard, your son was a good, decent, Christian man who paid a thousand times over for his moment of carelessness. If anyone ever learns of the nature of his illness, it shall not be from me, I can promise you."

"Thank you, Mr Hardiman. Truly, thank you." My host reached across and again took my hand in both of his. "And you will think about becoming a constable? There is little enough I can do for my dear boy now but at least I can care for those who cared for him."

Chapter Twenty-Nine

PORTER

"So this is where you spend your days, when you're not cluttering up the place at St Clement's," said a voice.

I looked up to see George Chapman leaning against the door frame of the stables. I put down the hoof of the horse that I was examining and used my shoulder to push the animal back into its stall. I closed the door on it and pulled it once to check; every ostler knows how quickly a horse can sniff freedom. I wiped my arm across my brow.

"Mr Chapman," I said.

"Mr Hardiman," he replied. He blew his lips out. "Phew – I thought my lodge was warm, but this now, well."

"Horses are warm animals," I agreed. "They keep me busy topping up their water in this weather, I can tell you."

"Talking of topping up," said the porter, jerking his head towards the inn, "what do you say to a dram? Are you permitted?"

"Better than that," I said. "Special prices."

I was grateful for those special prices, as it turned out that the porter of St Clement's had quite a thirst. Myself, I know from bitter experience not to mix drink with opium, and after our first tankard I made sure that the pot boy knew to dilute mine with plenty of water. George Chapman made no such request. After four tankards we were the best of friends, as he leaned towards me and threw an unsteady arm around my shoulders.

"And have you found our stolen paintings yet, Mr Hardiman?" he asked thickly. I must have looked surprised. "Oh, there's no secrets in a college." He winked and tapped the side of his nose. "They tell us to sit there, porters, day and night, winter and summer, and then expect us not to see anything." He drained his tankard again and shrugged. "It makes no sense, does it?"

I shook my head and beckoned again to the pot boy. "All water for me, lad," I said quietly as he leaned across me to collect the dead men.

Chapman slumped back in his seat. "When actually, Mr Hardiman," he lowered his voice to what he imagined was a whisper, "we see everything. Every thing and every body."

"I imagine you do," I said. "Fellows and college servants and tradesmen..."

"And women," he slurred.

"Women at St Clement's?" I asked. "But if the Master is a widower..." I stopped because the porter was shaking his head emphatically. "Not the Master?"

"Not the Master," repeated Chapman. He leaned forward to share his confidence. "The Bursar."

"Mr Galpin?" I asked.

"Shhhh!" said the porter, looking theatrically around the empty bar room. The pot boy returned and put two full tankards on the table, placing one carefully in front of me. I sipped it; water as requested. Chapman seized his own tankard as though it were the first and took a long drink before continuing. "Mr Galpin the Bursar has a lady friend," he said. "Very fine, she is too. Not one of your public ledgers, begging your pardon." He winked clumsily at me. "Elegant. But still..." He made a womanly shape in the air with his hands.

"His sister, perhaps?" I suggested. "His daughter?" The Master had already eliminated both possibilities but he might have been mistaken. If the Bursar was hiding anything from the Master, I suspected that the porter would know.

The porter shook his head, and then closed his eyes as the motion was starting to bother him. "Mr Galpin is a bachelor – no daughter. And his visitor is foreign – not a sister. I've heard her talk – accent. The Bursar is from Bristol." The porter laughed. "And she is most definitely not from Bristol." He stabbed the table with a finger to emphasise each word.

"Well, well," I said. "Still waters and all that."

"It's not right, you know," said Chapman after taking another generous drink. "Not natural. Not letting them wed. You can't be surprised if a man looks for female company."

"You have a point, Mr Chapman," I said. "How often does Mr Galpin entertain his lady friend, do you think?"

The porter paused, looking into the distance – I imagine his brain was struggling to work under these conditions. "A lot and then not much," he offered eventually. He tried again. "I think she visits Cambridge and then he sees her a lot. Then she goes away to London and he doesn't see her much. Aye, that's it." He looked pleased with himself.

"London?" I asked. "How do you know she goes to London? You said she was foreign – perhaps she goes home."

"Letters," said Chapman. "She sends him letters from London." He drained his tankard and very slowly fell sideways on the bench and started to snore.

Chapter Thirty

BURSAR

The next morning, I went to St Clement's. There was another porter on duty and he was happy enough to tell me that the Bursar was in his rooms. Once again I made my way to the wooden door, and this time there was an answer to my knock.

"Come in, come in," called a man's voice.

I went into the room, which was just as chaotic as on my previous visit. John Galpin was standing by the window, holding a book turned towards the light. He put a finger on the page to mark his place and looked across at me.

"Yes, Mr Hardiman?" he asked. He was noticeably less friendly than when he had wanted something from me. Perhaps he was regretting confiding in me.

"Good morning, Mr Galpin," I said. "I wondered if I might have a few moments to talk to you about a matter of some importance."

The Bursar raised an eyebrow. "Of importance to you, or to me?" he asked.

"Most definitely to you," I replied.

"You have found out something about the letter I showed you?" he asked. I said nothing. "Oh, very well," he said. He cast around for a scrap of paper to serve as a bookmark and put the book on top of an unstable pile on the floor. He then walked over to me, his false leg clapping on the floorboards. I wondered how the occupant of the room beneath this one coped with the noise. He held out his hand and I shook it. He looked around the room and walked across to two chairs by a table, clearing their seats by simply sweeping their contents onto the floor. "Please, make yourself comfortable, and tell me about this matter of importance."

"Thank you," I said, taking a seat. "I have not forgotten about your concerns regarding the death of Mr Perry. But today I need to ask you about something else: missing college property, and your foreign lady friend."

The Bursar sat back in his chair. "Well," he said. "You don't beat about the bush, do you?"

"You are an intelligent and busy man, Mr Galpin," I said. "I see no reason to waste your time."

"I am grateful, sir," he said. "And I shall pay you the same compliment." He took a deep breath. "The two matters are, as you have doubtless surmised, connected." He demonstrated by linking the fingers of his two hands, like a child playing the game of church steeples. "My lady friend, as you delicately put it, is Mademoiselle Marguerite Chastain. She is the daughter of a French chemist whom I knew as a young man; he was sadly killed during the wars and when his daughter visited England it was natural that she would seek the company and solace of a friend of her father's. At first it was just that, but as she grew into a beautiful woman..." Galpin shrugged. "The life of a Cambridge fellow can be a lonely one, Mr Hardiman."

"Could you not leave St Clement's and marry her?" I asked.

"I would be giving up a great deal, Mr Hardiman," he replied. "My livelihood, my research, my reputation as an academic, everything I have ever known as a fellow of St Clement's... And it has not seemed necessary." He cleared his throat. "Marguerite – Mademoiselle Chastain – is not like other young women. She is modern, independent," he searched for a word, "unshackled. She does not demand marriage."

"How convenient for you," I observed.

The Bursar flushed. "Not exactly convenient, no. There is a great deal of subterfuge – as you can imagine, our arrangement would not be condoned by many at the University."

"But still," I said, shrugging. "Many men would envy you. An attractive woman like that, willing to risk everything and to ask for nothing in return."

"Ha!" said Galpin. "No woman is content with nothing, Mr Hardiman. Marguerite is a well-travelled young woman, she has seen the fine things that life can offer, and I cannot refuse..." He stopped suddenly.

"And so you steal items from St Clement's to sell so that you can give her money," I said flatly.

"And there you are wrong, Mr Hardiman," said the Bursar. "I do not sell anything. Such a venture would be wrong."

I was taken aback. "What has happened to the missing items, then?" I asked. "The books? The paintings?"

"They are merely borrowed, to be used as security for loans," said Galpin.

"Taken to a pawnbroker, you mean?" I asked.

The Bursar looked aghast. "Nothing so vulgar, Mr Hardiman. A pawnbroker – the very idea. No: Marguerite has cultured friends who know the value of such items, and against them they are willing to extend credit to her." His face softened. "She has three young brothers to educate and a widowed mother who is sickly. She needs money to help them. My own resources are limited, but St Clement's has assets that it never uses and has all but forgotten. It is foolish and wasteful – immoral, even – that they should gather dust in a dark corner when good people are in such need."

Francis Vaughan stood, hands on hips, the very picture of indignation. "And so the Bursar has used – abused – his position, his trusted position, to steal from us," he said. "And then he sells these items – these priceless items of college history – to get money to support his... his..." He blew out his cheeks in frustration.

"His mistress, yes," I finished for him. "But he maintains that the items have not been sold – merely used as security for loans."

"And what does he propose that we do now, Mr John Galpin?" asked the Master. "Is there any chance he can recover the items?"

I shook my head. "He says not," I replied. "Although I daresay if you were to offer to repay the loans..."

Vaughan looked miserable. "St Clement's is not a wealthy college – we do not have that sort of ready money at our disposal. Would that we did. If only those coins had been found on our premises."

"The gold and silver dug up in Bene't Street last week, you mean?" I asked.

The Master nodded. "From the reign of James I, they say – astonishing." He thought for a moment, and then frowned. "And now I shall have to decide what is to be done with Mr Galpin. It is a delicate matter, as you know, with his family connections to the college. I trust this can remain between us..." He looked questioningly at me.

"For now, Mr Vaughan," I agreed. "After all, if the victim of the theft does not wish to take the matter any further..." He shook his head. "But if it becomes clear that there are other victims – that Mr Galpin has stolen from others – the decision will no longer be yours alone."

"Stolen from others?" said the Master, surprised.

I shrugged. "He has access to other valuable items," I suggested. "At the Philosophical Society, for instance – they have a library, I believe, and some interesting instruments."

Vaughan shook his head sadly. "I cannot believe that he would be so foolish." He sighed. "But then, had you asked me a month ago, I would not have believed he could steal from his own college."

"Very little that men do surprises me these days," I said.

"There is your philosophical side again, Mr Hardiman," said the Master. "I remember you told me you had been to New Holland – Australia. I daresay seeing something of the world will make a man philosophical about his fellows. You are not originally from Cambridge, I think – your accent is not local." He indicated the two armchairs and we sat down.

"No: I am from a village near Norfolk – you will not have heard of it," I said. "I left to join the army – a young lad in search of adventure."

"And you were in the Great War?" asked Vaughan.

I nodded. "In Spain and France," I said. "This is from Albuera." I indicated my face.

The Master grimaced. "The reports were terrible – horrifying."

"I was not sorry to leave the Continent," I allowed. But I was lying, of course; I had been heartbroken to leave Spain.

"And then?" asked Vaughan.

"And then we travelled to Ireland and Australia," I replied.

The Master shook his head, wondering. "After such excitement, what brought you back to England?"

"The officer I worked for became ill and wished to return home and I came with him – here, to Cambridge, last year," I replied.

The Master looked at me, surprised. "Last year?" he repeated. "Would that have been the poor Howard boy?"

It was my turn to be surprised. "Hardly a boy, but yes – Major William Howard," I replied.

“Indeed,” said Vaughan, “but then I knew him when he was a boy. His father and I are old friends. Mr Hardiman, once again I have cause to thank you – not just for the great service you did my dear friend, but also for making a decision much easier for me.”

“A decision, sir?” I asked.

“You have heard of the university constables that are soon to be appointed?” I nodded. “Each Head of House has been asked to put forward to least one name to recommend and I have been wondering whether you might be suitable, given the great service you have provided this college recently. And now that I am aware of the connection between you and the Howards, I need wonder no longer.”

Chapter Thirty-One

Ambition

I had just finished feeding the horses from the *Telegraph* and had propped open the door of the stables to try and cool the animals as much as possible after their sweltering journey. I turned from securing the canvas over the bales and jumped a little when I saw William Bird standing in the doorway.

"Good heavens, Will," I said, laughing. "You gave me quite a start, creeping up on me like that."

"There was no creeping, Gregory," said the innkeeper. "You just didn't hear me, chattering away to the horses like that."

"Ah, well," I shrugged. I waited. "How can I help you, Will?" I asked eventually.

"Do you have time for a stroll?" he asked.

"A stroll?" I repeated. William Bird was perhaps the hardest-working man in Cambridge, and afternoon strolls were not part of his day.

"A walk, then," he said. "Good heavens, Gregory – must I spell it out? I want to talk to you, but not here."

Ten minutes later we were skirting the edge of Butts Green, keeping in the shade of the trees and heading vaguely towards the river.

"Do you enjoy your work, Gregory?" Will said at last. "Working with the horses, I mean?"

"You know I do, Will," I said stoutly. "And if you're planning to bag me, just come out and say it. There's plenty of inns in Cambridge looking for a good ostler."

The innkeeper barked a laugh. "Bag you! Perish the thought. There's not a man in town to match you when it comes to horses, and we both know that." He stopped and looked at me. "It's about those other inns, really." He paused. "Look, Gregory, you know I'm not the sole owner of the Sun."

I nodded. "I do, yes: you are in partnership with Mr Mills."

"And have you seen Mr Mills recently?" asked Will. "At the inn? Around town?"

I thought for a moment and then shook my head. "I have not, no. Is he unwell?"

"Not physically, no," said Will, carefully. "But in his head... I blame myself – and Elizabeth certainly blames me."

"His wife? What does she blame you for?" I asked.

"For going into business with John in the first place," he replied. He kicked at the ground with the toe of his boot. "I trust you will not pass this on," he looked up at me and I shook my head, "but about ten years ago John Mills was in partnership with his brother Edward at another inn in Cambridge and they had to dissolve the partnership."

"They went bankrupt, you mean?" I asked.

Will shook his head. "Not quite – but they were only one step ahead of their creditors. John persuaded me that it was a youthful mistake – a lesson hard learned. But the truth is that John is no businessman. He has neither the head for numbers nor the stomach for risk. The Sun is struggling because of it. And it is making him ill. I called on him last week, and he said that he is not sleeping, and he complains of mental anxiety."

"I am sorry to hear it," I said, "but I fail to see..."

The innkeeper interrupted me. "Mr Mills and I have agreed to dissolve our partnership," he said. "The notice will be published soon."

"Where will you go?" I asked.

"Do you know Mr Bullen?" he asked in turn.

"The keeper of the Hoop?" I replied. I remembered my peculiar conversation with Mr Horwood.

"He is retiring from business," said Will, "and I am to replace him. As innkeeper of the Hoop." He could see the misgivings on my face. "I know that it seems something of a reversal of fortune," he admitted. "At the Sun we have four regular services – the *Telegraph*, the *Safety*, the *Tally Ho* and the *Wisbech Day*," he counted them off on his fingers, "while the Hoop picks up only scraps when other inns are full. But I have ambitions for the Hoop, Gregory, and I want you to come with me." He stopped again and turned to me. "Think of it, Gregory: a new adventure. We can take the poor old Hoop and build it up together. You're the best ostler in Cambridge, you've already told me as much – and drivers will go where their animals are most comfortable. I've my eye on pinching the Fakenham coach from the Black Bear, and maybe even the *Birmingham* from the Blue Boar. I can offer you a little more money – not much, mind." He laughed. "What do you say, Gregory? Do you fancy a move to Bridge Street?"

"There's something I should tell you before you make that sort of offer," I said.

"You're to be married," said Will flatly.

"Married? Good heavens, what gave you that idea?" I asked.

"It's more Hannah's idea than mine," he admitted. "She reckons that because you never bother the maids or eye up the ladies, you must have a secret sweetheart."

I laughed. "Well, you can tell your wife that there's no prospect of me getting married." A nearby clock chimed. "We'd better start heading back," I suggested, and we turned towards town. "Tell me, Will: have you heard of university constables?"

"University constables?" he replied. "I don't think so, no."

I repeated what Mr Howard had told me.

"Sounds like a good idea," said Will, nodding. "I've had some rowdy lads in the parlour in the past, but I can't lay a finger on them. It would be good to know I can call on someone a bit handy who can haul them out." He stopped and looked at me. "You, Gregory? You mean you're going to be a constable?"

"Just in the evenings," I said, "and only two or three evenings a week. I'll need to stay an ostler – I can't live on what they're going to pay a constable – but I'd need an understanding master, letting me work two jobs."

"From where I'm standing," said Will, smiling broadly, "things couldn't look better. I'll soon have the best ostler in town and my own constable on the premises."

Chapter Thirty-Two

GINGERBREAD

After the pageantry of the proclamation of the fair by both the town and the University, the Pot Fair was handed over to the people. Mrs Jacobs had been uneasy about it for a few days, watching the procession of traders, entertainers and hawkers making their way to Butts Green – or Midsummer Common, as some were now calling it – but once everything was in place and had received the blessing of the Mayor and the Vice-Chancellor, she was as keen to visit as anybody. She stood in the kitchen, checking her cap and then carefully putting her bonnet on over it. The bonnet, I knew, was much treasured and its appearance outside a visit to church showed how special the day was. She glanced at me.

"Very becoming, Mrs Jacobs," I said promptly. "Shall we?"

I had promised to accompany her to the fair so that she could meet her friend Mrs Wilson, who was walking in from Newnham with her husband.

It was yet another warm day, and we were grateful for the shade of the trees as we crossed onto Midsummer Common. Although it was not yet ten o'clock, the fair ground was already lively. Row upon row of stalls had been set up by traders to sell the goods they had brought in along the river – many of them with fine displays of the pottery that had given the fair its nickname. Mrs Jacobs stopped to inspect a large tureen, but I commented that she would have to carry it all day and would soon tire. The stallholder gave me a dirty look. At the end of each row of stalls was a beer tent, and to tempt the appetite there were plenty of hawkers. Saucers of hot peas were less popular than usual, thanks to the warmth of the day, but the gingerbread husbands and wives were selling well. Baked in wooden moulds in the shape of men and women and then covered in gilt paper, they smelt very tempting.

"When I was a girl," said Mrs Jacobs, nodding at a pile of the biscuits, "we were told that they were saints."

"I'm not sure it's quite holy to bite the head off a saint," I said, handing over a coin and choosing one husband and one wife, "but here goes." I gave the wife to Mrs Jacobs and then decapitated the husband with one bite. He was delicious.

Mrs Jacobs laughed. "Ah, there she is – Mrs Wilson!" she called, waving at her friend. "Thank you for your company, Mr Hardiman, and for the biscuit. I am sure you want to visit some of the other entertainments, and I shall be quite safe with Mrs Wilson and her husband."

As Mrs Jacobs had guessed, I was interested in some of the fair's more raucous offerings. For a few moments I stood and watched children being spun on a horse-driven merry-go-round. The plodding horse looked well enough, with a straw hat perched on his head, holes cut in it for his ears, and a bucket of water to hand. The children, depending on their character, either clutched in terror to keep their balance on their wooden mounts or waved madly at their mothers.

I moved away from the merry-go-round, finishing the last of my gingerbread, and headed towards a large tent with a banner across the top that promised "The Greatest Freaks on Earth!". Knowing only too well how it felt to be stared at, I had no wish to do the same to others. As I walked past, the ticket-seller called out that for a mere sixpence I could see a giant and a dwarf and a dancing dog. I turned my face to him so that he could see it clearly. He had the grace to go silent until I had moved away, and then started up his calling again.

The entertainment I wanted to see was further on still, towards the far edge of the fair ground: the boxing booths. As I had guessed, Zack Platten had brought some of his lads across the river to make some money by giving demonstrations and then to make more money by taking on any man foolish enough to think he could win against them in the ring. It was still early and so only two of the lads were sparring lightly in front of a sparse crowd. Alongside the boxing booth was a beer tent, and just coming out of it with a tankard in his hand was Zack. He handed the drink to a man watching the boxing and took a coin in exchange, then turned and caught sight of me.

"Gregory," he said with delight. "I wondered whether I would see you here. With your work keeping you in town."

"There's only the *Telegraph* going this morning," I said, "and Mr Bird said that as long as I prepared the horses before I left he would oversee the departure for me. I've no need to be back until the arrival of the *Wisbech Day* at half-past two. He's keen to keep me happy just at the minute." Zack raised his eyebrows but I shook my head. "I'll tell you when it's all settled," I said.

"Can I get you a drink?" he asked.

"Not during the day, thank you," I said, and laughed at how prim I sounded.

"Ah, but a fair day's not an ordinary day," said Zack. "Tell you what: I've some barley water – will that serve?"

"It will serve very well," I replied.

"You go over and watch the lads and I'll bring it out to you," he said. "By the way, how is it with those Greenway boys? Any trouble?"

"Nothing that has reached my ears," I said. "The thirty pounds for Mrs Ryder is due at the end of this month."

"Well, if they're late paying up and they need a little reminder," said Zack, smiling, "we'll send young Elias to have a word with them." He pointed at the two lads in the boxing booth. "The one in the blue neckerchief. He's very persuasive, is Elias." And just as he said that, Elias swung a swift punch and his sparring partner dropped to the ground like a sack of turnips. "Perhaps a little too persuasive at times."

Chapter Thirty-Three

PRIMER

Poor Jamie and I were sitting on two crates in the inn yard. The midday rush was over, the *Bury* was standing empty in the yard, the horses were resting in the stables, and Jamie was reading aloud to me. He had once seen me chuckling over a story in a newspaper and had asked about how I could make sense of the black marks on the page. In turn, I had asked Mr Giles the bookseller for advice and he had found me an old reading primer with pictures. And in our quiet moments, Jamie and I read together about the adventures of Pip the naughty dog.

"Hardiman," said a voice, and Jamie and I both looked up, shielding our eyes from the sun. Jamie gasped and stood up quickly, knocking over his crate and dropping his book. It was Jem Greenway.

I stood up more slowly. "No need to worry, Jamie," I said calmly. "Mr Greenway has come here to see me and to help Mrs Ryder. You remember Mrs Ryder?"

Jamie nodded slowly, not taking his eyes off Jem. "She wears a green hat," he said.

"That's right," I said. "Now you go into the kitchen, Jamie, and fetch a jug of water for us. I'll have a quick word with Mr Greenway, and then we can read more about Pip."

"But he's... a bad man," said Jamie, turning to me and speaking in a loud whisper. "He might hurt you."

"Out of the mouths of babes," I said, looking at Greenway. He had the grace to look uncomfortable. "If he gives me any trouble, Jamie, I shall yell for you. I promise."

Jamie thought for a moment and then walked towards the kitchen, pausing at the door to turn and give Greenway a hard look.

"The lad's a cork-brain," growled Greenway, stooping to pick up the reading primer.

I held out my hand for it. "Yes, but a cork-brain who knows enough to want to improve himself," I said. Greenway gave me the book. "And the thirty pounds?" I asked.

Greenway's face darkened. "You don't waste time, do you." He reached into his coat pocket and pulled out a grubby purse. He weighed it in his hand for a moment and then passed it to me. I opened the drawstring and peered inside. "Thirty sovs," he said. "You can count them."

"Oh, I will," I assured him. "Gold sovereigns aren't much use to Mrs Ryder, but I'll change them here for her." I pulled the drawstring closed and put the purse into my own coat pocket. "For next month's payment, you'll find me at the Hoop."

"Been bagged, have you?" sneered Greenway.

I ignored him and sat down on my crate again, not least to hide the trembling in my legs. As Jamie had observed, Jem Greenway was a bad man. After a few moments, he turned and left.

Chapter Thirty-Four

Moving

William Bird stood under the gallery in the yard of the Sun, sweat dripping from him. He took the kerchief from his neck, wiped his face with it and sighed mightily. I looked up at him from my position seated on a barrel, hands on my knees.

"I must be mad, Gregory," he said, shaking his head. "Of all the days to move across town, I choose today."

"You weren't to know how hot it would be," I pointed out.

"That's true," agreed the innkeeper. "And we couldn't move before the end of term." He went over to the horse trough and dipped his kerchief into the water, wrung it out and draped it once more around his neck. "What do you reckon?" He looked around at the boxes, crates, baskets and bundles piled up in the yard. "Three more loads?"

"About that," I said, getting to my feet. "Here's the cart now. I'll wipe down the horse and give him a drink while you see to the loading." The cart turned into the yard and I took hold of the bridle to make sure that the driver stopped with the sweating animal in the shade.

Two hours later it was all done. The Hoop was barely a hundred and fifty yards from the Sun as the crow flies, but its outlook was very different. Instead of the Great Gate of Trinity College, the Hoop looked out at a row of elegant but serviceable buildings on Bridge Street. And, as Will had pointed out several times already, it had a much more convenient location on a corner, to catch people coming from the north, south and east. Moreover, its yard was larger than that of the Sun, and – as he showed me – the loft above the stables was properly furnished with a stump bed, a table with two chairs and a stand for a washbasin.

"You could live in," he said hopefully as we both stood in the loft, but I shook my head.

"I'll work all the hours you need," I said, "but I need to see the open fields."

"Trust me to choose a country boy," said Will, but he smiled. We climbed down the ladder and went into the inn. He had grand plans for his new venture.

"Imagine it," he said, sweeping his arms wide as we went into the bar room which looked out onto Bridge Street. "Bigger windows, to let in the light and so that passersby can see us and know that we have nothing to hide. Fresh paint, and clean up this old woodwork. The large parlour upstairs," he pointed upwards, "it's clean enough, but we could do more with it."

"Will you allow the coroner to carry on using it?" I asked, thinking back to George Ryder's inquest.

"Of course," said Will. "People come to an inquest when they might not otherwise come into the Hoop. They see how clean and fresh it is, they have a drink, they get good service, their horse is well tended," he tilted his head at me, "and before you know it they're staying here for a night before taking the coach to London, or coming here to attend a musical evening, or watch a play."

"Musical evenings?" I said. "And plays?"

"Oh yes," said Will, his eyes shining as he looked off into the distance. "I think I should repaint the front, to let people know that the Hoop is changing. What do you think of this: the Hoop Inn and Family Hotel. Something for everyone."

"Humphh," said a woman behind us and we both jumped. Hannah Bird stood with her arms folded over the large apron she had put on to cover her clothes, an old scarf wound about her head to protect her hair. "There won't be anything for anyone unless you get a shift on, William Bird. Musical evenings and repainting can wait until we've unpacked everything. And unless you'd care to address yourself to a crate, Mr Hardiman..."

I gave Will an apologetic look and left him to his fate. You won't blame me, I am sure.

Chapter Thirty-Five

CONSTABLE

When I told Mrs Jacobs that I was to be appointed a university constable, she imagined – and described to me, in great and unwanted detail – a grand ceremony with fine robes and golden regalia. As it was still so hot, I was horrified at the prospect of putting on heavy robes with ermine linings. But thankfully Mrs Jacobs was being fanciful, and when the instruction came it was simply to attend the Vice-Chancellor Thomas Le Blanc in his rooms at Trinity Hall, where he was Master.

The porter at the gate pointed the way to me, across the first court, into the principal court, and then through the dining hall passage into the back court. The Master's Lodge was on my left – a handsome, pale stone building with crenellations. I knocked at the door, explained my business to the footman who answered, and was shown into the Master's study. By now I was familiar enough with such rooms to expect the usual muddle of books and papers. But having been trained as a soldier to keep only those possessions I really needed, and to keep them neat, I confess I wondered how these great academic minds could order their thoughts in such messy surroundings. As I looked around me, I suddenly realised that the Master himself was there, sitting in a grand chair by one of the open windows. With not a fine robe or ermine lining in sight, he wore his plain black academic gown over a dark outfit.

"Mr Hardiman?" he called, beckoning me over. "Forgive me, sir, if I do not rise – I am a martyr to the gout, as you can see." He indicated his leg, propped up on a stool and with the foot swaddled in a large bandage. "My medical man tells me that keeping it elevated is the thing, but it still pains like the Devil. When it's bad, the only comfort is a good swig of port, but that's the very thing that makes it worse. A cruel dilemma, sir." He shook his head sadly.

I held up my hands to stop him rising. "Please do not get up on my account, sir," I said. "Yes: Gregory Hardiman." I leaned forward and we shook hands.

"To be sworn as a constable, if I am not mistaken," said the Master, turning to a pile of papers on the table at his elbow and leafing through them. "Ah yes, here we are: Gregory Hardiman. Be a fine chap, would you, and go to the door and call for my clerk. He's in the office to the right – Mr Elkins."

I did as he requested, and stood to one side as a very small, very crooked, very elderly man inched his way out of the office and walked slowly over to the Master.

"Mr Elkins," said the Master, "this is Mr Hardiman. He is here to be sworn as a constable."

The clerk turned his head slowly to look at me. "Who has summoned a constable?" he asked.

"Not summoned – sworn," said the Master, raising his voice. "Sworn!"

"Ah yes," said Elkins, nodding. "We will need the ledger." He turned slowly to return to his office.

"I should have thought to mention it before, to save him the journey," said the Master. "Never mind: we can find plenty to discuss. Now, Mr Hardiman, have your duties been explained to you?"

"In the broadest terms," I said.

"And have you seen the Act?" he asked.

"The Act?" I echoed.

"The Act creating the constables," he elaborated. "Quick: catch up with Elkins and tell him to bring the Act as well."

Just then the door opened and the Master's footman appeared, ushering another man into the room.

The Master leaned forward to see who it was. "Come in, come in, Hustler." A tall, elegant man with silvering hair put down a large leather bag by the door before walking over to shake first the Master's hand and then mine. Like Le Blanc, he was wearing plain academic dress, but on him it looked like the most stylish of choices. Le Blanc looked up at me. "Mr Hustler is the Registrary of the University," he explained. "He keeps us in order – a thankless task, I am afraid. And today he is required to witness your swearing in. Hustler, this is our new constable, Mr Hardiman."

By now Elkins was making his way slowly back to us, and of course I had not told him to bring the Act as well. So once more he turned away.

Le Blanc and I caught each other's eye and smiled. "I often wonder whether he was appointed by Robert de Stretton himself," he said. "The first Master of this college – in 1350."

"You are wicked, Le Blanc," said Hustler in a gentle Suffolk accent entirely at odds with his smart appearance. He glanced around the room. "And when are you going to tidy this room? It is a wonder to me that you can find anything at all."

Le Blanc shrugged and smiled. "I can't, sir – and that is precisely why I keep the ancient Elkins."

The clerk finally returned, holding both a ledger and a piece of parchment. Hustler looked around and chose the least cluttered table in the room. He lifted a few piles of papers and books from it to clear space for the clerk to put down the ledger and arrange a pen, inkstand and pounce pot alongside it. The clerk then held out the parchment to the seated Master, who waved it away and pointed at me. I took hold of the parchment. "Read that," he instructed. "Aloud, if you please. We need to be sure that you can read, Mr Hardiman."

I glanced at him; he smiled and nodded encouragingly. I cleared my throat and began. "An Act for the better preservation of the peace and good order in the universities of England. Fifth July 1825. Whereas it is expedient to add to the means anciently provided..." I stopped, as Hustler held out his hand.

"You can read, Mr Hardiman – thank you," he said, and I handed him the parchment. "Do you have the oath, Mr Elkins?" he asked.

The clerk heaved open the ledger on the table. Tucked into it was a piece of paper. He held it out in a bony hand and I walked over to take it. Elkins sat down at the table, took up the pen, dipped it and readied himself to write.

"Do you require me to stand, Hustler?" asked Le Blanc. "Only..." he gestured at his bandaged foot.

"No need, no need," said Hustler. "Now then, Mr Hardiman, hold up your right hand, yes, that's it, and read the oath aloud, if you please."

I did as I was told. "I, Gregory Hardiman of Radegund Buildings, Jesus Lane in the county of Cambridge do swear that I will well and faithfully execute the office of constable within the precincts of the University of Cambridge during my continuance in office, that is to say until the thirtieth of September 1826, unless I shall be sooner dismissed therefrom by the Chancellor or Vice-Chancellor for the time being of said university. So help me God."

"That date," said Le Blanc, pointing at the paper I was holding. "Slightly longer this year. The normal term of appointment will match that of a Proctor – that is, from the beginning of October to the end of September of the following year. You can serve for more than one year but you must swear the oath annually."

"I understand," I said, returning the oath to the clerk.

"And now we must sign the ledger," said Hustler. "Who is to go first, Mr Elkins? Mr Elkins?" Le Blanc indicated with his hand that Hustler should speak up. "Shall we sign now, Mr Elkins?" he all but bellowed.

"Indeed, sir," said the clerk. He held out the pen first to me. I walked over and saw my name inscribed in the ledger, fifth in a list of eight headed with the word Constables – none of the other names was familiar to me. Elkins pointed to a space below where he had written, in a beautiful clear hand, the day's date. I signed my name as carefully as I could. I handed the pen to Hustler, who added his signature; it was surprisingly untidy, and he swore quietly as he smudged the final letter. Finally, the clerk carried the ledger and pen over to Le Blanc, who reached up and signed. Elkins returned to the table, sprinkled pounce on the page, waited a moment, blew off the powder and then carefully closed the ledger. We all watched in silence as he returned to his office.

"And now for your regalia, Mr Hardiman," said the Registrary, walking over to the bag he had brought in. From it he took first a truncheon which he handed to me. About twelve inches long and made of dark wood, it was richly and brightly painted with both the Royal arms and that of the University. I felt its weight and lightly hit my palm with it. "You are to carry this at all times when on patrol," he instructed. "It is to be used as a weapon only in extremis, but it serves to identify you as a constable of the University. It is your authority, Mr Hardiman." He reached into the bag again and struggled to withdraw a much larger item. "And this," he said at last, shaking out a dark item of clothing, "is your cape." He indicated that I should turn around and he placed it over my shoulders. It was a huge thing: made of heavy woollen stuff, it covered me from the neck to the ground, with plenty beyond that. I was boiling. "It's more for ceremonial wear," explained Hustler. "The tail is for when you are mounted. Not that you will often be on horseback. Good heavens, man, take it off before you expire."

I gladly shrugged off the cape and draped it over my arm. "Mr Hustler," I said, "may I ask what you meant about ceremonial wear? I thought my job was to patrol the streets with a Proctor."

"And so it is, Mr Hardiman," said the Registrary. "But this is the University, and we cannot function without ceremony, you know." He gave me a smile that was surprisingly mischievous. "Nothing to alarm you. Every Sunday during term, four constables will attend the University Sermon with the Proctors."

"At Great St Mary's?" I asked.

"Of course," confirmed Hustler. I silently gave thanks that my late mother would never know that her good Catholic son would be kneeling alongside Protestants. "And whenever a Proctor attends a Congregation – you know, conferring degrees and undertaking other university business – he will be attended by two constables. With eight of you, you will be able to take it in turns. And now I must go, gentlemen." He smiled again, picked up his empty bag, nodded to us and left.

"And then there were two," said Le Blanc. "Now, Mr Hardiman, we should toast your appointment. I imagine you would like a large port, and it would be ill-mannered of me not to join you."

Chapter Thirty-Six

AUCTION

Some people think that the town of Cambridge is no more than the University. They assume that outside term we simply go to sleep and wait for scholarly life to resume and wake us. But since the undergraduates had vanished at the end of term a month ago, much had happened to me: I had moved from the Sun to the Hoop and had been sworn in as a constable. Granted, I had yet to undertake any duty at all as a constable – nothing would be required of me in that capacity until the start of Michaelmas term in October – but still, it was a change.

And as I walked along Trinity Street towards Nicholson's, Cambridge was far from asleep. After the violent gales of Friday last, there were still broken tiles and fallen branches scattered about the town. Mrs Jacobs had once again feared for our roof, and indeed the groaning of the wind had been alarming at times, but our sturdy building had stood its ground. I passed a street sweeper and moved out of his way as he prodded savagely at the gutter with his broom.

"Plenty to keep you busy today," I observed.

He stopped sweeping and looked up at me. "It's all very well, the town spending its money on gas lighting," he spat out the words, "and paving," again, said with contempt, "but then along comes

Mr Purchas, all grand, waving to the crowds, and what happens?" I shook my head. "This happens." He pointed at the street. "Filth and rubbish – they bring it with them and drop it for me to sweep up." He shook his head. "He might be mayor again, for the third time, thank you very much, but I tell you, Mr Purchas, he has no idea. None at all." And he started sweeping again, even more vigorously.

I smiled and walked on to the bookshop. Mayoral elections were often rowdy affairs – if a man's candidate wins he will drink in celebration, and if he loses he will drink to forget – and so I had avoided the town the day before, instead going for a long walk out into the countryside. And now, with a few extra shillings to my name thanks to my constable's retainer, I was calling on Geoffrey Giles in the hope that he might recommend some poetry for me. With the library at the Bull Book Club I am able to read many books that I could not possibly afford, but from time to time it is a great pleasure to buy my own small volume. I like to inscribe my own name on the flyleaf, I like to underline the words that are new to me and copy them into my vocabulary book. I had a quick look at the display in the window before pushing open the door.

Giles was behind the counter and smiled warmly at me.

"Mr Hardiman," he said. "How fortuitous. I have just acquired a book that I thought you might enjoy; I was going to bring it with me on Wednesday evening but now you have saved me the errand." He ducked down and reappeared with a very slim book in dark red covers. "It is not new, mind you, but a good copy – very sound and all but unmarked." He handed it to me. "Thomas Gray. I know you enjoy his churchyard elegy."

"Their homely joys and destiny obscure," I said.

"Indeed," said Giles. "Well this," he put his hand on the book, "is two of his odes. A little more laboured, shall we say, than the elegy, but still, you might enjoy them."

I took the book from him and opened it. I read a few lines and looked up at the bookseller. "Helicon?" I asked.

Giles frowned slightly. "A mountain in ancient Greece," he said. "Oh, and a river, I think. Does either of those make sense?"

I nodded. "The river. 'Helicon's harmonious springs'. It's certainly more... learned than the elegy. Plenty here for my vocabulary book. How much is it?"

"Three shillings," he replied. "If you like, you can take it now, see what you think, and either return it or pay me when we meet on Wednesday evening."

"Thank you," I said. "I shall take good care of it."

"I know you shall," he said. He paused for a moment, checking that we could not be overheard. Mr Robinson, the other bookseller, was at the top of a ladder on the other side of the shop, carefully taking out books one by one to dust them, and there were no other customers. "Tell me, Mr Hardiman," said Giles in a low voice, "are you still concerned about those London booksellers? Your missing volumes?"

I nodded. "I sent enquiries to two of them, but have heard nothing. Perhaps a personal visit would be more fruitful."

"I doubt it, Mr Hardiman," said Giles.

"Do you know something, Mr Giles?" I asked.

The bookseller came out from behind the counter and beckoned me to follow him to the rear of the shop. He held open the curtain leading to the back room and ushered me through it, following me in and then indicating that I should take one of the chairs. He retrieved something from his satchel hanging on the coat hook and then sat down opposite me.

Wordlessly he handed me a sheet of paper he had taken from his satchel. "Auction," it said at the top of the sheet in heavy, dark letters. "Catalogue of valuable, rare and splendid books, excellent prints and curious manuscripts." I looked up at the bookseller and he raised his eyebrows. I continued reading. "To be sold by auction, by Mr Wakefield, at his house at No 83 Pall Mall on Friday 22 July and the three following days (Sunday excepted)." I read it again quickly. "Last month," I said.

"Last month," confirmed Giles. He handed me a pamphlet. I glanced at it and looked up at him. "The advertisement came to me by chance," he explained, "used as wrapping on a book sent to me from London last week. As soon as I saw it, I sent word to a friend down there and he managed to find the catalogue. All too late, of course, but at least it confirms, well, you will see. Lot number 37."

I leafed through the dense text of the catalogue, the first two pages explaining the conditions of sale, followed by a numbered list of some two hundred lots in the auction. I ran my finger down the list until I came to lot number 37. "John Wallis," I read aloud. "*Opera Mathematica*. First edition." I looked up at the bookseller and he nodded. "Four volumes bound in three, handsomely finished in calf. Complete with four engravings and three portraits. Large bookplate in each, showing the volumes to be the property of ABN. Imprinted in Oxford in 1593, 1595 and 1599." I stopped. "But the volumes taken from St Clement's had the college crest in them."

"All too easy to cover up with a bookplate," said Giles sadly. "A large bookplate, apparently applied by a suitably anonymous owner. 'ABN' tells us nothing definite."

"So you think..." I left the question unfinished.

"It would be too great a coincidence," said the bookseller. "This is a rare work, one of the monuments of mathematics," he waved his hands in the air to show great height, "and to have one go missing and another turn up at an auction sixty miles away within months, well, they cannot be but one and the same."

I thought for a moment. "Do we know if the *Opera* was sold?" I asked.

"Sometimes a catalogue will be a complete record of a sale," said Giles, holding out his hand. I passed the catalogue to him. "But this one has very little in it. See," he opened it and pointed. "There are two or three lots on this page with a mark against them, but on other pages there is nothing. Perhaps whoever had this catalogue was interested only in particular lots. And the *Opera Mathematica* would be beyond the purse of most buyers. There is nothing marked against it in here."

A thought occurred to me. "Actually, the buyer is less important – at least, for now," I said. "What we need to know is who was the seller. Who put the *Opera* into the auction?"

"I had a similar thought," agreed Giles. "Unfortunately, the sale was not held by one of the more reputable auctioneers – Mr Sotheby, for instance, or Mr Evans. These gentlemen, I am sure, keep meticulous records of all items bought and sold. But Mr Wakefield – this is not a name I know. We may be lucky, or we may not. Either way, I have already sent an enquiry to the friend who found the catalogue for me. We shall just have to be patient, Mr Hardiman."

Chapter Thirty-Seven

TIDYING

I will admit that my feet dragged a little as I walked to St Clement's a week later. I had grown to like Francis Vaughan and was sad at the thought of having only bad news for him.

Chapman the porter was sitting outside his lodge, leaning against the wall and with his face turned to the sun. He opened one eye as I let the college gate close heavily behind me.

"Mr Hardiman," he said. "Watch your step as you go round the corner; there's a large branch come down a week ago and I'm still waiting for the woodman to chop it up." He closed his eye and then opened it again. "I assume you're here to see the Master."

"I am," I said. "Is he in?"

"In his rooms," said the porter, "tidying up." And he laughed at the surprise on my face.

The windows in the Master's beautiful room were wide open, allowing the warm air to blow through. Every pile of papers had a book or heavy ornament placed on it, and in the middle of the room stood the Master himself, gown and coat removed, shirtsleeves rolled up to the elbow, and an open book in his hands.

"Mr Hardiman," he said, turning to me with a smile. "You will be astonished to see that I am tidying my room. The trouble is, every book I pick up to dust and put away seems so very interesting, and I promise myself that I will read just a couple of pages, and, well, here I am." He shrugged and closed the book he was holding. "It's the same every summer, I am afraid. The best I can hope for is to keep it at the same level of chaos from year to year – to stem the tide, as it were. Now, how can I help you?"

"Is Professor Sandys in college?" I asked.

"Ah – so you have some news for us about our missing books," he said happily, but then he saw my expression and his face fell. "But it is not good news."

"I am afraid not," I said.

The Master sat down with a sigh. "Out with it, then, Mr Hardiman," he said.

I too sat down. "First, sir," I said, "I must confess that I have had to take someone else into our confidence, someone more familiar with the trade in books. But you must not worry: Mr Giles is entirely trustworthy and has no truck with gossip. No-one will hear from him that St Clement's is involved."

"Geoffrey Giles?" repeated Vaughan. "At Nicholson's?" I nodded. "I know the man, and you are entirely right about his character."

I felt much relieved. I then explained what we had learned about Mr Wakefield's auction, and said that Mr Giles had sent word to London to make enquiries into the identity of the seller.

"And he found nothing," said Vaughan flatly. "The seller was using a false name, or was represented by an agent who has vanished into the ether."

I nodded. "Not only that," I said, "but no trace can be found of Mr Wakefield the auctioneer. The room he used for the auction, at 83 Pall Mall, was simply hired for the duration of the sale. The landlord is the Board of Ordnance, but it seems that it was a private arrangement made by one of their staff – and no-one is owning up to it."

"The Board of Ordnance?" repeated Vaughan. "The supplier of munitions to the army and navy?"

"When the mood takes them," I replied, thinking of those long weeks we camped in Spain, praying that muskets and powder would reach us before Boney's troops did. I continued. "Mr Giles is of the view that the location for the auction was chosen very carefully. Number 83 Pall Mall was once the location of Mr Christie's auction rooms, and number 93 is still where Mr Evans holds his sales."

"And so this Mr Wakefield," he looked at me questioningly and I nodded, "Mr Wakefield hoped that people would associate the address with reputable auctions."

"It seems to have worked," I said. "The doorman remembers the sales being well attended on all four days." I reached into my pocket and took out my notebook. "Here we are," I said, running my finger down a page that I had marked with a slip of paper. "Wakefield – paid cash for room rental – no address given. Auction lots delivered two days before first day of sale."

"To allow people to inspect them before bidding," interjected the Master.

"Aye," I agreed. "No register kept of visitors to the auction. Unsold lots collected the day after the end of the auction by Wakefield's sister. Doorman had no recollection of Wakefield, but said his sister was a well-rigged frigate." Vaughan's eyebrows shot up. "A well-dressed and handsome woman," I explained.

"As she can afford to be, with a brother who has just made a tidy sum from selling stolen books," said the Master grimly. He pressed his forefingers to his temples. "To summarise, Mr Hardiman," continued, "we know that a first edition of Wallis's *Opera Mathematica* was sold in London last month. Mr Giles thinks it likely to be the one stolen from us. But everyone involved in the sale – the seller, the buyer, the auctioneer and his well-rigged sister – used a false name or has simply left no trace. Do I have it right?"

I nodded sadly. "Yes, sir," I said.

"All that remains with regard to the *Opera*, then, Mr Hardiman," said Vaughan, "is to hope that whoever has bought it knows what he has, and treats it with respect."

"How will you tell Professor Sandys?" I asked.

"Perhaps we should be thankful that Professor Sandys is not in Cambridge," said the Master. "He had a fall just after the end of term and I insisted that he go to stay with his niece in Edinburgh to recuperate. He was not best pleased; apparently she is a woman of a determinedly dour nature." He smiled, but sadly. "Between us, Mr Hardiman, I fear that Professor Sandys may not return to Cambridge."

"I am sorry to hear that, sir," I said, and I meant it. I was even more sorry that I had a further revelation for the Master. "There is something else, sir," I said. I took a deep breath. "The doorman in Pall Mall, he did remember one visitor very clearly. Thanks to his wooden leg." I glanced down at my open notebook. "A tall handsome man, full head of grey hair, wooden leg that made a clapping noise as he walked."

Vaughan pushed himself up out of his chair. "The fool," he blurted. "The blasted fool. To risk so much." He strode to the door and back again. "He leaves me with no choice." He frowned. "No choice at all. I shall have to remove him."

Chapter Thirty-Eight

CHAMBERMAID

As William Bird had noted, business was slower at the Hoop than at the Sun, and I was using the time between coaches to visit other inns in town with a view to pinching some of their trade. I was just walking past the Blue Boar when I heard a young woman call my name. Peeping around the gate to the hotel's yard was Agnes.

"Hello, Miss Agnes," I said, touching my forelock. She giggled. "What are you doing here?" I asked.

"Oh, I didn't like the new people at the Sun," she said. "It's not the same now that you and Mr Bird have gone. So I heard about a job here," she indicated the building, "and here I am. But not for long."

"And why's that?" I asked.

"I'm hoping to be married," she said, smiling shyly.

"To a young gentleman called Charlie Grantham?" I asked.

Agnes's mouth fell open. "How did you know that?" she asked.

I touched my nose. "Ah, there's not much gets past me, you know," I teased her. "But he seems a good, steady sort, and I hope you'll be very happy. You'll not go thirsty, anyway."

Agnes laughed. "I'll save you a piece of the bride cake," she said.

"Agnes," I said, a thought suddenly occurring to me, "do you work in the laundry here?"

She stood up a little straighter, and indicated the white pinafore she was wearing. "I'm a chambermaid now, Mr Hardiman. Cleaning the rooms, making the beds, hanging up the clothes."

"Very impressive," I said. "So you see the guests and know a little bit about them."

Agnes leaned towards me. "More than a little, sometimes, Mr Hardiman," she whispered. "Some of them, well, they don't take care to hide much, if you know what I mean."

"Tell me, Agnes," I said, lowering my voice as well. "Have you seen a well-dressed, elegant woman, aged about thirty, with pretty dark hair and a French accent. Mademoiselle Chastain."

Agnes's eyes shone. "Oh yes – all the chambermaids know her! She has the loveliest clothes, and her perfume, we all..." She suddenly looked guilty. "You won't tell, will you?" I shook my head. Agnes looked over her shoulder then made her confession. "We all have a quick dab of it when we're cleaning her room. Here." And she held out her wrist. It smelled of vanilla.

"So Mademoiselle Chastain is staying here now?" I asked.

Agnes nodded and then frowned. "But that's not her name – Chas – what did you say?" I repeated it. Agnes shook her head. "No: she's Madame something... Laccra?"

"Madame?" I said. "So she is married?"

Agnes nodded. "We all think it's funny." She leaned towards me again. "Her husband always has the room next door to hers, with a door between them. Madame told Lizzie – she's head chambermaid – that it's because he snores like a warthog. You wouldn't know it to look at him – proper dapper, he is. Lizzie has a name for him: she calls him the elegant gent from Ghent. That's in Flanders – where they come from. She's quick like that, Lizzie." The nearby church bell started to toll and Agnes jumped. "Heavens, here I am chattering away, and there's still three rooms to be done. I won't forget that piece of bride cake, though." And she ran back into the yard.

Chapter Thirty-Nine

PACKING

From outside the Bursar's door, and despite the thick oak between us, I could hear the sounds of John Galpin preparing to leave Cambridge. There were thuds and crashes as heavy items were moved, and snapped orders given to his footman. I knocked loudly on the door. The footman opened it.

"Please tell Mr Galpin that Mr Hardiman is here to see him," I said.

A moment later the footman returned. "You're to go in, and I'm to leave you alone, thank God," he said, and all but ran down the stairs.

I walked into the Bursar's rooms. The man himself was standing by several toppling piles of books, with three large trunks open in the middle of the room. He glanced at me and then continued his packing, if that word could grace simply throwing books into trunks.

"Mr Hardiman," he said flatly. "You will not be surprised to see me leaving Cambridge."

"I am not, sir, no," I admitted. I stood silently as he threw in another half-dozen books.

He looked up at me again. "Well?" he asked rudely. "Surely you are not a man to gloat."

I shook my head. "I wonder if I could tell you something. Something that might help you."

"Help me?" he said with a dry laugh. "I doubt that, Mr Hardiman. All my years of work," he swept his arm, taking in the room and the whole of Cambridge, "finished. My ambitions – gone. I shall live out my years teaching dull-witted schoolboys in Bristol." He spat out the final word.

"What I have to tell you may not change that," I said, "but I think you should know everything before you leave Cambridge."

That caught his interest. He put a last handful of books into one of the trunks and then wordlessly pointed at a chair. I sat down and he carried over another chair to sit near me. As he sat, he stretched out his wooden leg and rubbed his thigh.

"Your lady friend," I started. "Mademoiselle Chastain. You told me that she is the daughter of a friend of yours. A French chemist."

"Pierre Chastain," he agreed.

"And Mademoiselle Chastain told you that her father had died on the battlefield," I continued.

He nodded. "At Marengo," he said.

"And you believed her?" I asked. The Bursar looked startled. "I mean, did she have the look of her father? Did she know things about him that only a daughter would know?"

"She was a baby when he died," said Galpin, almost to himself. "She knew where he grew up and how he and I had met..." He looked at me. "You had best explain, Mr Hardiman."

I sat up straighter. "Mademoiselle Chastain's real name is Madame Sophie Lacroix," I said, "and she is not French: she is from Brussels. She is the wife of an art dealer in Ghent, in Flanders. And I fear that she and her husband have been working with a man here in Cambridge to entice you to take items from St Clement's in order to please her. Their plan all along has been to sell the items rather than using them as security for loans." I stopped. "As I believe you saw at an auction in Pall Mall last month."

Galpin stared at me. I suddenly wondered whether I had been wise to call on him alone. A man backed into a corner is always dangerous.

"Madame Lacroix has been taking you for a fool," I said quickly.

The Bursar blinked. "So she is nothing to do with my old friend Chastain?" he asked. I shook my head. "Not French?" I shook my head again. "Who is their man here in Cambridge?" he asked. I hesitated. "Surely I am entitled to know who has conspired to ruin me?" he said. Suddenly he looked horrified. "Dear God: is it the man who killed Perry?"

"There may be a connection," I said, choosing the word carefully. "It may be that Mr Perry had threatened to expose your... activity, and they feared that this would put paid to their plans."

"But enough to kill a man?" asked the Bursar, aghast. He stood and paced around the room, looking at me from time to time. I let him take in what he had heard. "And you will not tell me his name?" he asked at last.

"It would be unwise," I said. "Nothing is certain – yet."

"But if he has killed once to protect his, his – game," he said, his voice rising, "and now you have told me about Madame Lacroix, surely I am in danger myself?"

"It's possible," I admitted. "Perhaps it is time to take the matter to the magistrate."

"You do what you want," said Galpin, flinging another few books into one of the trunks and slamming down its lid. "I am not staying here, waiting for him to find me. I shall be on the night coach from the Black Bear to London, and then I shall travel as quickly as I can to the Swan with Two Necks to catch the Bristol coach."

"You would do better to wait for the *Tally Ho* tomorrow morning at eight o'clock from the Sun," I suggested. "It goes direct to the Swan."

"And spend another night here in Cambridge, so that this murderer can finish his work with me? I think not," said the Bursar. "And now, if you please, Mr Hardiman, I am very busy."

Chapter Forty

TRANSACTIONS

Even though the bells had already chimed ten o'clock, there were still traces of light in the sky. I was relieved to get out into the cool evening air; the evening's talk at the Bull Book Club had been interesting, but with so many people in the small room it soon became stuffy and I had struggled to keep my eyes open. I felt a hand on my shoulder.

"Mr Hardiman, do you have a minute?"

I turned. "Mr Fisher," I said, genuinely pleased to see him. "Of course: shall we walk together?"

He looked up at the sky. "Yes," he said. "But not straight home, I think. Shall we cut through to Coe Fen – I feel in need of fresh air."

We headed south, quietly companionable. The banker indicated with his hand and we turned right down Little Saint Mary's Lane, heading for the river and the open land. There was a gentle rustling and quiet cheeping as the birds settled for the night in the trees in the churchyard.

"I hear that Mr Galpin has been asked to leave St Clement's," said Fisher eventually.

"I believe it became impossible for the Master to do anything else," I said carefully.

We turned into the field and found the path alongside the river.

Fisher breathed deeply. "The thefts, you mean?" he asked. I looked at him but said nothing, and he stopped. "Nothing stays hidden for long in Cambridge, you know," he said. "It is fairly common knowledge that Galpin had a mistress. And it is very common knowledge that having a mistress involves expense. Add to that the fact that the porter of St Clement's likes his drink..." He raised his eyebrows at me.

"Ah," I said, understanding. "There's no secrets in a college, that's what he said to me. The porter. It's an odd thing, this college life."

"Hah!" said Fisher. "I agree, but what makes you say it?"

"If I stole something from the Hoop – a bale of feed, say, or a barrel of beer," I explained, "my master would report me to the magistrate. But Mr Galpin – a man in a far more trusted position who steals things that are far more valuable than animal feed or beer – well, he is simply asked to leave quietly and we'll say no more about it. It doesn't seem right."

"And no more it is, Mr Hardiman," said the banker. "But what you need to understand is that there is little that a Cambridge college dreads more than scandal. No family is going to entrust their son to a college that has a reputation for immorality. Particularly not the nobility – and they pay the highest fees, as you know. And so the Master of St Clement's will not report his bursar to the magistrates. He will simply instruct him to leave."

"But what about the Bursar's family?" I asked. "Mr Vaughan told me that Mr Galpin's grandfather gave an important legacy to the college. Won't they ask questions if he leaves?"

"You don't forget much, do you, Mr Hardiman?" said the banker. "My guess is that the Master will agree with them to keep the whole thing quiet, as long as they make good the losses the college has sustained. After all, Galpin's family will not want a scandal either."

"So the family will pay for the missing items and the Bursar will quietly disappear from Cambridge," I said. "Is that it?"

"Almost," agreed Fisher.

"Almost?" I repeated.

"I have been undecided about telling you this, Mr Hardiman," said Fisher, looking down at his feet and shuffling awkwardly. "We bankers are meant to be utterly discreet." He paused and I waited. "But I am not sure we should simply let Mr Galpin walk away, and I would value your opinion."

"I will give it if I have one," I promised.

"Shall we walk as far as the ladders and then turn back?" he suggested. "Not that I am suggesting a dip in the river at this time of night." We walked for a minute in silence until the banker spoke again. "Mr Galpin is a customer of my family's bank. Has been for many years, ever since he arrived in Cambridge. And initially his account looked just as you might expect: deposits of lecture fees, his annual stipend as bursar, occasional ad hoc payments from St Clement's for expenses incurred – the usual. And then cash withdrawals for personal expenditure – again, the usual. But about a year ago it started to change." The banker stopped and looked at me, anguish on his face. "I should have said something sooner. But the thought of my brother mocking me and saying yet again that I don't understand the business of banking, well, I was afraid to mention it."

"To mention what?" I asked.

"Large sums of money – larger than before – larger than Galpin should have had. Being put into his account and then withdrawn a few days later," said Fisher.

"And this has been going on for about a year?" I asked. He nodded. "Large sums?" He nodded again.

The banker thought for a moment. “I could check the records,” he said. “We would have a note of where the money was sent from, to be paid into Galpin’s account.”

“Or you could ask Galpin himself,” I said. “If there is an innocent explanation then he has nothing to hide.” I could see Fisher considering the matter. “I couldn’t ask him, of course, but his banker – well, that would be different,” I suggested. “And I know exactly where he’s going to be right now.”

We were both puffing by the time we ran into Market Street. The lamps were still blazing at the Black Bear and we could tell from the calls of the driver that the coach for London was preparing to leave. We ran into the yard and stood on tiptoe to look into the coach. It was full, but none of the people inside was John Galpin. I backed away and looked at the men sitting on the outside; the Bursar would not normally choose this, but if space were scarce – but again, no sign of him.

I turned to Fisher. “He definitely said he would catch the night coach, and here it is. Shall we check the parlour?”

But just then the driver, already in place on his box, lifted his whip and called out, “Away!” The horses leaned into their stays and the coach jerked into movement. If Galpin had intended to travel to London this evening, he had missed his chance. Perhaps he had taken my advice to go on the morning coach instead.

Chapter Forty-One

SHIRTSLEEVES

It was only a matter of weeks since William Bird and I had quit the Sun, but already I could see the difference. The yard was untidy and unswept, and when I poked my head into the stables to say hello to the new ostler he was nowhere to be seen. I glanced at the clock on the wall – it was already gone seven o'clock and with two coaches departing at eight, the place should have been busy with activity. Still, it was no longer my business, and I sat on an upturned crate to wait for George Fisher. We had agreed to meet at half past the hour to try to have a word with John Galpin before he left for London.

Just then I saw George Chapman walk past the open gate towards Bridge Street, doubtless on his way to St Clement's. I called out a good day to him and he came into the yard.

"I thought you had left this place," he observed, looking puzzled. "Moved over the way." He jerked his head in the direction of the Hoop.

"I have," I said. "I am waiting to have a word with Mr Galpin before he boards the *Tally Ho* to London."

Chapman looked surprised. "Mr Galpin the Bursar?" he asked.

"Of course," I replied. "Do you know of any other Galpins in Cambridge?"

"No need for that," said the porter. "I didn't realise he was going to London, that's all. When he left college last night, he gave orders for his trunks to be sent to Lynn so I thought..."

I stood up quickly. "Lynn?" I asked. "Are you sure?"

The porter drew himself up to his full height. "Mr Hardiman," he said, "as porter of St Clement's College I have been dispatching gentlemen's trunks to every part of this country and beyond for more years than I care to remember, and if someone tells me to send a trunk to Lynn then that is precisely where it will go. I am quite sure of it."

I put a hand on his shoulder. "I meant no offence, truly – I am just surprised to hear it. Thank you, Mr Chapman – you have been a great help."

I had just rounded the corner by Nicholson's when I spotted Fisher walking along St Mary's Lane towards me. I waved at him and walked quickly to meet him, and explained what I had learned from Chapman.

"I spoke to the driver," I finished, "and Galpin has not booked a place on the coach. He knew him, when I mentioned the leg."

"So if he's heading to Lynn," said the banker, "he could go by road or by packet."

"I've thought of that," I said. "The packet doesn't go until to-morrow morning at nine. And the coach leaves the Black Bull at half past two this afternoon."

At that moment the church bell chimed the half hour. "Half-past seven," said Fisher. "The earliest Galpin can leave – unless he has his own horse, and with his leg I think that's unlikely, or has hired a coach, which seems an unnecessary expense – is in," he counted on his fingers, as a banker should, "seven hours' time." I nodded.

"And we know from the porter that he has quit his rooms at St Clement's." I nodded again. "So where will our bursar spend those seven hours?"

"I may have an idea," I said. "Do you happen to know where Mr Robert Horwood lives?"

Fisher looked surprised. "Horwood? From our book club?"

"Yes," I said. "I believe that he and Mr Galpin know each other quite well, and it's possible that Mr Galpin might want to bid him farewell before leaving."

The banker looked at me. I could tell he wanted to ask more. "Mr Horwood's lodgings?" I asked quickly.

The town was going about its business as we strode out along Trumpington Street towards New Town. After about ten minutes we reached Gonville Cottage and turned left onto Downing Terrace. The road was filled with builders and their carts and materials. Helping to meet the demand for new houses was William Wilkins, a well-known local architect, who had had the idea of developing New Town. He had built himself a fine home called Lensfield, and then sold off some of its garden to build a short terrace of neat, bright homes called Annesley Place. And according to Fisher, Robert Horwood had leased number 5 Annesley Place – the last in the terrace. The curtains were open, suggesting that the household was awake.

I pulled the bell pull and we heard the bell ring inside, but no-one came. I pulled again.

"Someone's in the back room," said Fisher, who was peering in at the front window. "I just saw them push the door closed."

"Round the back, then," I suggested.

We walked down the side of the house and into the back garden; it was yet to be tamed. As we drew level with the window of the back room, I saw movement inside and waved urgently at Fisher to duck down. We waited a moment and then lifted our heads slightly so that we could see in. Standing at the sink in his shirtsleeves and splashing his face and hands with water from a basin was John Galpin. The door to the back room – which was obviously the kitchen – opened and in walked a woman wearing a dressing gown and with her hair loose. She looked at something on the floor and screamed, which made me jump. She saw me and pointed. Galpin turned to look.

"Go for help," I said to Fisher, without turning my head. "Quickly!" From the corner of my eye I saw him backing away.

The back door was thrown open and there stood Galpin, wiping his hands on a cloth. "Mr Hardiman," he said. "How you do get about the town. You had better come in." Something in his eyes made me uneasy. "Now, Mr Hardiman," he said sternly, and I did as I was told. I was concerned for the woman, and with a bit of luck I would be able to keep him talking and calm until help arrived. I soon realised my mistake, as he stood to one side and I walked into the house. "In there," said Galpin, pointing to the kitchen. The woman had disappeared – I assumed to get dressed – and lying on the floor in a pool of blood was Robert Horwood. I heard a click as Galpin locked the back door.

"Ah yes," he said conversationally, coming into the kitchen behind me and closing the door. "He just would not listen to reason. Unfortunate, but there you are."

Horwood was, like Galpin, in his shirtsleeves. He was on his back on the floor, one arm flung out and the other hand over a bleeding wound in his gut.

"You've just missed him," said Galpin. I had seen enough staring faces and glassy eyes on the battlefield to know that he was right.

"Do take a seat, Mr Hardiman." I pulled out one of the three chairs at the table – the one furthest from the spreading blood – and sat down. All the while I kept my eyes on Galpin, who returned to the sink and dipped his hands once more into the basin of water. He was humming to himself.

The kitchen door opened and the woman came back in. She had dressed her hair and was wearing a dark red travelling outfit. She was very pale and her eyes were huge in her face, but she was trying hard to master herself.

"Sophie, my dear," said Galpin, for all the world as if I had made a social call, "I am not sure you know Mr Hardiman. Mr Hardiman is an ostler. That means he cares for horses at an inn." He turned from the basin and leaned against the counter, looking at me. "You know plenty about Madame Lacroix, of course. Her English is excellent, but not flawless," he said, as though the woman were not in the room. "Some of the more unusual words still puzzle her." He turned to Madame Lacroix. "And now, my dear, we must decide what to do with Mr Hardiman. He has seen..." he gestured about the room, "all this."

Madame Lacroix's eyes darted to mine. "I am sure Mr Hardiman will see the wisdom in saying nothing," she said.

"Are you, my dear?" asked Galpin in a teasing tone. "Then you have a more trusting nature than mine." He reached over and stroked her cheek; I saw her shudder but she stood her ground and even smiled at him.

"None of this is Mr Hardiman's business," she said. "We have taken nothing of his," she looked at me and I shook my head, "and he has no particular amitié – affection – for Mr Horwood." Again I shook my head. "I am sure that for a small consideration, Mr Hardiman will forget that he was ever here and simply go about his business as an ostler. Caring for horses." She smiled brightly, but with her lips only. "Come, chéri, it is time for you to dress." She held out a hand. Galpin looked at her.

"No," he said decisively, standing up straight. "No: I am afraid he will have to join Horwood." He turned and reached into the basin, and I saw that he had a knife. He wiped it on the cloth and then walked over to me, that infernal leg clapping on the floor. I was scrambling to my feet when there was a hammering at the back door and a more distant thumping at the front. Galpin looked over me out of the window into the garden and I ducked under his arm. There was a splintering sound as someone broke down the back door and a second later a large man in a blackened overall appeared in the kitchen. He lunged for Galpin just as Madame Lacroix kicked the Bursar in his good leg, and Galpin dropped the knife and collapsed to the floor.

Fisher burst into the kitchen. "Hardiman," he gasped, "are you wounded?"

I held out one hand and put the other to my heart, which was racing. I shook my head. "No, no – not at all."

Two more men appeared behind Fisher; I guessed they had come in through the front door. I looked around.

"The woman," I said. "Madame Lacroix – where is she?" The four men all looked at each other.

"We left the front door open," said one of the latecomers. I pushed past them and raced down the hallway. Coming towards the house, marching Madame Lacroix in front of him, was Chapman.

"Ah, Mr Hardiman," he called. "Were you hoping to catch Mr Galpin's lady friend before she left town? I have done it for you."

"Mr Chapman," I said, astonished. "How did you come to be here?"

"No doubt I shall be in trouble for it at college," he said, steering his captive to the front door, "but when you left the Sun this morning, all mysterious, I knew something was afoot, and so I followed you. Good job I did too. Now, now, miss," this to Madame Lacroix, who was struggling in his grip, "I think you'd best give in gracefully, don't you. You're going nowhere."

We went indoors and found that Fisher had moved everyone out of the kitchen and into the parlour at the front of the house. Galpin had put on a coat and was sitting in an armchair, the two unknown men flanking him, each with a firm hand on his shoulder. The larger man in the overall had gone.

"Ah, Madame Lacroix," said the banker politely. "Perhaps you and," he looked at me and I supplied the name, "you and Mr Chapman could sit on the sofa."

The woman said nothing and did as she was told. Chapman and the two other men nodded at each other. Fisher indicated that I should step out into the hall with him.

"Who are they?" I asked in a low voice.

"Porters from Peterhouse," he said. "It was the nearest college – porters are always useful. And the big chap, well, that was just lucky. He's a coalman and he was making a delivery to the college – I thought he looked handy and I promised him a few shillings for his help."

"Where is he now?" I asked.

"I've sent him to the town gaol," he replied, "to warn Mr Payne that we shall be bringing him a couple of guests. He'll look after them until they can be brought before the magistrates at the next Quarter Sessions."

"Is there anyone in Cambridge you don't know?" I asked.

"Even a gaoler needs a bank account," said Fisher. "I expect he'll send a coach to collect us – it wouldn't do for anyone to see the bursar of St Clement's being marched along St Andrew's Street to the gaol."

Chapter Forty-Two

COLLUSION

George Chapman heaved open the college gate and stepped inside, holding it open for me. The night porter who had stayed at his post when Chapman sent word that he had been delayed was snoozing quietly on the chair outside the lodge. Chapman turned to me and held out his hand. I shook it.

"Thank you for your help today, Mr Chapman," I said. "If you hadn't followed me, well." I shrugged.

The porter winked at me. "Just as well I'm a nosy one, isn't it?" he said. He shook the shoulder of his sleeping comrade. "Wake up, Sam – I'm parched. Put that kettle on the stove, there's a good man."

I lifted my hand in farewell and walked around the court to the Master's staircase. The clock on the chapel was showing just before four o'clock, and now that Chapman had mentioned it I realised that I was thirsty myself. Perhaps the Master could be persuaded to send for some of that excellent coffee. I climbed the stairs wearily; after the excitement and tension of the day, my legs were heavy and unsteady. I knocked on the door and the footman answered. He took one look at me and said the single word, "Coffee." He stood aside and ushered me into the Master's rooms, announcing me before disappearing down the stairs.

Mr Vaughan walked quickly across the room to me, holding out his hands. He took hold of me and steered me to the most comfortable armchair in the room, all but pushing me into it. He then stood over me, looking at me appraisingly, before going to the sideboard, uncorking a decanter and pouring a glass of dark liquid. He brought it over and handed it to me.

"Port," he said. "Sip it. Good for shock. Coffee is on its way, I imagine – William looked full of purpose."

He picked up a nearby chair and placed it near me, then sat and waited quietly, smiling encouragingly. I had no choice. I drank the port. The door opened and the footman came in carrying a tray on which was a pot of coffee, two cups and a plate of slices of cake. He set down the tray on a nearby table.

"Pour the coffee, if you would, please, William," said the Master. "And is that fruit loaf?"

"It is, yes, sir – still warm," said the footman, pouring a steaming cup of coffee and passing it to the Master. "Do you need anything else, sir?"

"I think we are well taken care of, thank you, William," said the Master, passing the cup to me.

William wrapped a napkin around the pot of coffee to keep it warm and left the room.

"While you drink that," said Vaughan, "and eat this," he handed me two slices of fruit loaf on a plate, "and gather your strength, I shall tell you what I know. I have received a message from Mr Payne at the town gaol, saying that he has Mr Galpin and a Madame Lacroix under his care. They are to be taken before the magistrates and that will determine what happens next. Had their actions – their alleged actions – concerned only the University, it would have been a matter for the Vice-Chancellor's court, but that is not the case. It is, as they say, out of our hands. Now, how is that coffee?"

"Very good," I mumbled through a mouthful of fruit loaf. I had realised that I was starving and couldn't stop myself. The Master noticed and wordlessly put another slice on my plate before refilling my cup. I ate that one too, before sitting back in the armchair. "Thank you," I said. "I have had nothing since breakfast."

"I guessed as much," said Vaughan. "And now perhaps you can tell me what happened."

I related to the Master the events of the day, from my first attempt to find the Bursar at the Sun, to the frightening episode in the house in New Town, and finishing with the conveyance of Galpin and his mistress to the town gaol. Vaughan listened in silence, nodding occasionally.

When I had finished, he spoke. "Madame Lacroix is the woman that the porters have seen visiting Mr Galpin's rooms," I nodded, "the one who wears vanilla as a scent. And she was going by the name of Mademoiselle... Chastain. Is that right?"

"Yes," I agreed, "but we were wrong when we thought that she was fooling Mr Galpin. He knew all along who she really was – he helped her concoct that story about her being the daughter of a French chemist he had known. And as for all those clankers about collateral for loans – I was a fool to believe him."

"We both wanted to afford him the benefit of the doubt, Mr Hardiman," said the Master sadly. "But he simply told more and more lies – clankers, as you have it. I wonder why."

I shrugged. "You know the Bursar far better than I do, sir," I said. "My guess would be that he thought it would make Madame Lacroix seem more pitiable, someone he might want to help out of the goodness of his heart..."

"And the property of St Clement's," added Vaughan grimly.

"Indeed," I said. "I can see that a jury might be more sympathetic to a man who steals in order to help the woman he loves, rather than, well, rather than a deliberate scheme to, to..." I struggled for the word.

"Collude?" suggested the Master.

"Collude," I said with satisfaction. "That's exactly the word. A deliberate scheme to collude with her to bleed money and property from the college." I quickly took my vocabulary book from my pocket and noted down this pleasing word.

Vaughan smiled at me. "From the Latin *colludere* – to play with. But now with a more sinister meaning."

I added this explanation and returned the book and pencil to my pocket.

"And do we know what they were planning to do, had you not caught up with them in New Town?" continued Vaughan.

"Oh yes," I said. "Mr Galpin seemed to think that the gaol would offer only a temporary halt to his plans and told us exactly where they were going. Madame Lacroix tried to stop him, but he just talked and talked. I did wonder whether his mind had...." I stopped to remember how Galpin had seemed completely unaware of the change in his fortunes. "They were going to travel together to Lynn, taking a final few items with them, and then board a boat to Antwerp. Apparently there is a friendly captain who, for suitable remuneration, is happy to pretend that Madame Lacroix is his sister and the Bursar her husband."

"And what of the other man's part in all this – Harwood?" asked the Master.

"Horwood," I said. "Robert Horwood." I shook my head. "He thought he was in charge, when in reality he was being used. According to Galpin, Madame Lacroix had met Horwood and thought that he could be useful to them – and let him believe that he had had the idea to force the Bursar into stealing in order to keep his mistress."

"But why involve Horwood at all?" asked Vaughan.

"He had useful connections for selling the items, I think," I said. "Especially the books, given his membership of the Bull Book Club. And then he dragged his younger brother into it – your man of business."

"Poor chap," said the Master. "He paid a high price for it."

"I wouldn't feel too sorry for either of them," I said. "Just because a man is outsmarted by someone even more devious, it does not excuse his attempts."

"Do you think Horwood found Mr Wakefield – the book auctioneer?" asked Vaughan.

"Almost certainly," I replied. "And I think it more than likely that Wakefield's comely sister was Madame Lacroix, keeping an eye on him – and, more importantly, on the profits from the auction."

"Perhaps Madame Lacroix might be persuaded to shed some light on the fate of the *Opera Mathematica*," said the Master.

I shrugged. "If it meant that the judge would look more kindly on her, I daresay she would hand over her own grandmother. Madame Lacroix is a woman who knows precisely the value of everything, including information."

Vaughan shook his head. "There, Mr Hardiman, you are wrong," he said. "She may know the price of everything, but the value, well, that is something else entirely."

CONCLUSION

SOME TIME LATER

As you have stayed with my tale this long – for which I thank you – you would no doubt like to know the outcome. But before you shake your head too much and throw down this book in frustration, I should warn you that you may not feel that justice has been served. For my part, Major Howard once told me that I am a realist – that I see things as they are rather than wishing for them to be different. That's not to say that I don't have hope, but rather that I don't let the unfairness of the world weigh on me. Given what I have seen, it is just as well.

But to our story. John Galpin tried the patience of poor Mr Payne for several days, talking incessantly and demanding all manner of fine treatment, until a physician arrived from Bristol. He had been sent by the Bursar's family and after spending some time with Galpin he applied to the Home Secretary Mr Peel and was granted a warrant to transfer his patient to Brislington House asylum in Bristol. Mr Relhan, who reads the medical journals, tells me that this is a forward-thinking place for wealthy lunatics. As a curious man, Galpin should find much to interest him there.

Madame Lacroix was less fortunate in her family. Her husband – Agnes's elegant gent from Ghent – melted into the Continental mists. Whether he was really her husband, or simply a dealer making sure of his investment in her, we shall never know. Sophie Lacroix stood trial alone, on various counts of fraud, and was sentenced to transportation for seven years. I know better than most what awaits her in Australia, but if anyone can make a success of life in that harsh world, I daresay she can.

With no-one left to mourn them, the Horwood brothers were buried together. Robert Horwood's friends at the Bull Book Club contributed to a fund to erect a stone on their grave; I myself gave five shillings.

Talking of money, you will be pleased to hear that Jem Greenway has kept to our arrangement and pays me five pounds each month to hand on to Mrs Ryder. He is not happy about paying it, but then neither is she happy about needing it.

The Master of St Clement's, Francis Vaughan, is performing the duties of bursar while trying to find someone else to take on this thankless task. Sadly, apart from the genuflecting angel that James Horwood handed over in the parlour of the Hoop, St Clement's has not recovered any of its stolen items. The new librarian – an energetic young fellow called Anthony Reeves – is currently delving into all corners of the college and drawing up a detailed inventory of every work of art and every book in the place. George Chapman is tolerating him.

GLOSSARY

Money

In the 1820s, nearly all money that Gregory would have encountered was in coin form. There were banknotes, but these were for large denominations and would not have been in common usage for people of his class and limited wealth.

The coins that Gregory would have handled are these (in ascending order of value):

- Farthing (a quarter of a penny)
- Halfpenny
- Penny
- Sixpence
- Shilling (twelve pence)
- Half crown (two shillings and sixpence)
- Crown (five shillings)
- Sovereign (a gold coin worth a pound, or 240 pennies)

You may also have heard of a guinea – this is one pound (i.e. a sovereign) and one shilling.

As for the actual spending value of these denominations, of course that changes as our modern currency values fluctuate. But at the time of writing – summer 2023 – here are some approximate exchange rates:

- A penny in Gregory's time would buy what would cost us about 30p today
- A shilling would buy about £3-worth of goods today
- A sovereign would buy about £60-worth of goods today.

So when Gregory buys a month's worth of opium for two shillings, he is paying about £6.

Anglesey leg – an artificial leg, made of a wooden shank and socket, steel knee joint and articulated foot controlled by catgut tendons running from the knee to the ankle; invented in London in 1816 by James Potts, it became known as the "Anglesey leg" after the Marquess of Anglesey, who lost his leg in the Battle of Waterloo and wore the leg

Bagged – sacked, dismissed from work (apparently from the idea of a worker being told to put his tools into his bag and leave)

Barouche – a large, open, four-wheeled carriage, heavy and luxurious, with a collapsible hood over the rear half, and drawn by two horses

Boney – the contemporary (and slightly contemptuous) nickname for Napoleon Bonaparte

Bouncer – a bully

Chincough – whooping cough

Clanker – a lie, usually quite a big and harmful one

Cork-brain – light-headed, foolish person

Cross – if something is done upon the cross, it is done illegally or dishonestly (as opposed to upon the square)

Cut-throat inn – a public house of the roughest nature, often frequented by criminals and prostitutes

Dead men – empty bottles, glasses or tankards

Fadge – slang for a farthing, or a quarter of a penny

Gull – to cheat or dupe (hence "gullible")

Half seas over – almost drunk, very tiddly

Joskin – a countryman, an unsophisticated and simple rustic person, a bumpkin – used as a derogatory term

Landau – a luxury carriage with seats facing each other over a dropped foot-well, and a soft top that could be folded back, and drawn by two or four horses

Mace – to mace a shopkeeper, or to have goods upon the mace, is to obtain goods on credit that you never intend to pay for

Mardle – a gossip or a chat [Norfolk]

Maw / mawther – a young woman or girl [Norfolk]

Mill – to fight; to mill someone is to beat him up

Miniscule – what we now call lower case in lettering, as opposed to majuscule, or upper case or capitals

Nib – a gentleman or person of high rank

Noddy – a simpleton, a harmless fool, a silly fellow

Palm – to bribe or give money for a service or information [Regency]

Phaeton – a light four-wheeled carriage for two people, with open sides in front of the seat and front wheels smaller than the rear, and drawn by one or two horses

Pounce – a light powder (historically made from cuttlefish) sprinkled over ink to help it dry, in the days before blotting paper

Psalter – a book containing the Book of Psalms and perhaps other devotional material (such as a liturgical calendar), usually illustrated, either with full-page pictures (aristocratic psalters) or with miniature pictures in the margins (marginal psalters)

Public ledger – a prostitute (because, like that document, she is open to all parties)

Quarter Sessions – the Courts of Quarter Sessions were the meetings of two or more magistrates (also known as Justices of the Peace) to hear and determine criminal cases, to remit capital offences and other serious felonies to the next Assize Court, and to administer local government (the Quarter Sessions were held at least four times a year, hence the name)

Ribbons – the reins of a horse's bridle

Shanks' pony – to travel by Shanks' pony is to use your own legs, i.e. to walk

Sizar – in the days before entrance examinations, bright boys could be recommended by their schoolmasters to attend the University and apply for a scholarship once in residence; in exchange for their board and tuition, they were required to wait on High Table in their college dining hall, and were fed on High Table leftovers – perhaps the most famous Cambridge sizar was Isaac Newton

Slavey – a derogatory term for a servant

Sovereign – a gold coin introduced in 1817 and valued at one pound

Square toes – an old man, as they are fond of wearing comfortable shoes with room around the toes

Staithe – quay [Norfolk, and still in regular use today]

Stirrups – someone who is up in the stirrups is flush with money, riding high

Stump bed – a bed without posts (i.e. a cheaper and plainer bed than the four-poster)

Tick – to have something on tick is to have it on credit, i.e. before paying for it (short for “ticket”)

Titty-totty – small, compact, dainty [Norfolk]

Up in the stirrups – see *Stirrups*

Upon the mace – see *Mace*

Upon the cross – see *Cross*

Yard butter – in a practice unique to Cambridge, sellers of butter would weigh out a pound and then roll it out into a long cylinder between two flat boards each a yard long. These cylinders would then be sold on the market or taken door to door, and people would buy by the length rather than the weight – so a nine inch length would give you a quarter-pound. The advantage was that the seller did not have to use a whole range of weights – a simple ruler was sufficient. The "yard butter" died out with the introduction of rationing in the First World War.

Yelp – to complain, and in particular to complain vociferously about something actually quite trifling

University Structure

For readers who are not familiar with the organisational and command structure of Cambridge University in the 1820s, here is a very brief overview.

The ceremonial head of the university was the **Chancellor** – chosen for his ability to bring fortune and favour to the university. He did not reside in Cambridge or exercise day-to-day power, and so the head of the university for all practical purposes was in fact the **Vice-Chancellor**. He was one of the "head of houses" – heads of the colleges, who might be known as masters or principals – and was chosen by them from their own number every 4 November, to serve for a year. In 1825 – the year in which this book takes place – the Vice-Chancellor was Thomas Le Blanc, a lawyer and Master of Trinity Hall. The duties of the Vice-Chancellor included managing university finances and estates, deciding on prizes, holding authority in Cambridge city government, granting licences, deciding in matters of discipline, and opening Stourbridge Fair each September, as a prelude to the academic year.

Each college had its own command structure. At the top of the tree was the head of house, usually known as the **Master**. He had oversight of all college affairs – administering its property, seeing to the learning and good conduct of its members and presiding over meetings of college fellows – but he left most financial concerns to the **Bursar**. The Master received a good income and was provided with a gracious lodge in college grounds. He would also receive a dividend from the profits of college estates. Crucially, heads of houses were the only senior members of the university who were permitted to marry. In the 1820s, this small number of dignitaries and their wives formed Cambridge's upper class society of mixed-gender dinner parties and morning calls.

The teaching staff within a college were known as **fellows**. They had rooms assigned to them within the college and lived and dined within its walls. The students were known as **scholars** or **undergraduates**. Some lived in college – often in a "set" composed of a bedroom and a sitting room – and some lived out in lodgings.

One of the fellows would serve as the college **Bursar**. It was often a thankless task, and finding a fellow willing to do it was sometimes tricky. The job of the bursar was to oversee college finances, with money coming in from leases and rents on college properties (buildings and extensive agricultural land), and money going out to maintain the college and its inhabitants. In the time period covered by the Gregory Hardiman books – 1825-1830 – college finances, and therefore the job of the bursar, were becoming more complicated. Bursars were expected not simply to take in college income and make payment for college expenses, but also to make sound investments to secure the future of the college. Many of them were not up to the task.

AFTERWORD

Thank you for reading this book.

If you liked what you read, please would you leave a short review on the site where you purchased it, or recommend it to others? Reviews and recommendations are not only the highest compliment you can pay to an author; they also help other readers to make more informed choices about purchasing books.

ACKNOWLEDGEMENTS

This book is the first in a planned series of five, and as such I have had to do an enormous amount of research in order to get my cast of characters and my locations in place from the outset. And in doing so I have taken shameless advantage of the deep knowledge and boundless patience of a huge number of people. And here they are...

Richard Reynolds, crime fiction expert – for suggesting a Cambridge series in the first place, and the members of our **Crime Crackers** book club for keeping my nose to the grindstone by regularly asking how the book was going

Lucy Lewis (University Marshal), **Tim Milner** (Pro-Proctor for Ceremonial) and **Seb Falk** (Senior Proctor) – for their expert insight into the role of the university constable, past and present

Melissa Kozlenko (Curator of the Royal Anglian Regiment Museum at Duxford) and **Justin Saddington** (Curator of the National Army Museum in Chelsea) – for their help with understanding the history of Gregory's regiment

Catherine Collins, **Tony Kirby** and **John Pickles** of the Cambridge Antiquarian Society – for expert guidance on local maps and changing street names

Sally Kent (Department of Archives and Modern Manuscripts at the Cambridge University Library), **Rosalind Grooms** (Cambridge University Press Archivist) and **Jacqueline Cox** (Keeper of University Archives) – for helping me to untangle knotty bits of University history

Genny Silvanus (Archivist at Corpus Christi College) – for letting me delve into her college's accounts from the 1820s

Robin Payne (former Hospital Archivist) and **Mark Wilson** (current Hospital Archivist) – for explaining what happened to dead bodies pulled from the river

Yvonne Fisher – for writing a terrific thesis on coroners and their work

Richard Clammer (Paddle Steamer Preservation Society), **Paul Richards** (True's Yard Fisherfolk Museum in King's Lynn) and **Luke Shackell** (King's Lynn Borough Archivist) – for providing vital details about the steam packet service between Cambridge and Lynn in the 1820s

Mary Burgess, **Mike Petty** and **Tamsin Wimhurst** – for being the best local historians that any community could hope to have

James Keatley – for preparing a superb military service record for Gregory

Azucena Keatley – for giving Gregory an intriguing yet credible life in Spain

Helen Hollick – for winning my reader competition to create a college motto for St Clement's

Professor Philip Hardie – for translating Helen's motto into flawless Latin

Numerous anonymous users of the **TheNapoleonicWars.net** forum, who so generously discussed possible injuries and traumas for poor old Gregory

Roy McCarthy – for being, as always, a simply sterling beta reader

I am extremely grateful to you all for knowing so much and then agreeing to share that knowledge and your time with me. Thank you.

And if despite this wealth of world-class assistance I have made errors, they are entirely my own.

REVIEWS

Praise for *Fatal Forgery*

"I loved the sense of place, with some surprising revelations about jail and courthouse conditions and operations, and an interesting change of setting at one point, which I won't reveal for fear of spoiling the plot. There was great attention to detail woven skilfully into the writing, so I felt I learned a lot about the era by osmosis, rather than having it thrust upon me. All in all, a remarkable debut novel."
Debbie Young, author and book blogger

"From the start of this story I felt as if I had been transported back in time to Regency London. Walking in Sam's footsteps, I could hear the same cacophony of sound, shared the same sense of disbelief at Fauntleroy's modus operandi, and hung onto Constable Plank's coat tails as he entered the squalid house of correction at Coldbath Fields. I am reassured that this is not the last we shall see of Samuel Plank. His steadfastness is so congenial that to spend time in his company in future books is a treat worth savouring."
Jo at Jaffareadstoo

Praise for *The Man in the Canary Waistcoat*

"Susan Grossey is an excellent storyteller. The descriptions of Regency London are vivid and create a real sense of time and place. Sam Plank, Martha and Wilson are great characters – well-drawn and totally individual in their creation. The dialogue is believable and the pace well fitted to this genre. The novel shows excellent research and writing ability – a recommended read."
Barbara Goldie, The Kindle Book Review

"Regency police constable Sam Plank, so well established in the first book, continues to develop here, with an interesting back story emerging about his boyhood, which shapes his attitude to crime as an adult. This is not so much a whodunit as a whydunit, and Grossey skilfully unfolds a complex tale of financial crime and corruption. There are fascinating details about daily life in the criminal world woven into the story, leaving the reader much more knowledgeable without feeling that he's had a history lesson."
Debbie Young, author and book blogger

Praise for *Worm in the Blossom*

"Ever since I was introduced to Constable Sam Plank and his intrepid wife Martha, I have followed his exploits with great interest. There is something so entirely dependable about Sam: to walk in his footsteps through nineteenth century London is rather like being in possession of a superior time travelling machine... The writing is, as ever, crisp and clear, no superfluous waffle, just good old-fashioned storytelling, with a tantalising beginning, an adventurous middle, and a wonderfully dramatic ending."
Jo at Jaffareadstoo

"Susan Grossey not only paints a meticulous portrait of London in this era, she also makes the reader see it on its own terms, for example recognising which style of carriage is the equivalent to a 21st century sports-car, and what possessing one would say about its owner... In short, a very satisfying and agreeable read in an addictive series that would make a terrific Sunday evening television drama series."
Debbie Young, author and book blogger

Praise for *Portraits of Pretence*

"There is no doubt that the author has created a plausible and comprehensive Regency world and with each successive novel I feel as if I am returning into the bosom of a well-loved family. Sam and Martha's thoughtful care and supervision of the ever-vulnerable Constable Wilson, and of course, Martha's marvellous ability, in moments of extreme worry, to be her husband's still small voice of calm is, as always, written with such thoughtful attention to detail."
Jo at Jaffareadstoo

"Do you want to know what a puff guts is or a square toes or how you would feel if you were jug-bitten? Well, you'll find out in this beautifully researched and written Regency crime novel. And best of all you will be in the good company of Constable Sam Plank, his wife Martha and his assistant Constable Wilson. These books have immense charm and it comes from the tenderness of the depiction of Sam's marriage and his own decency."
Victoria Blake, author

Praise for *Faith, Hope and Trickery*

"What I like about the delightful law enforcement characters in this series is their ordinariness. They are not superheroes, they do not crack the case in a matter of a quick fortnight, but weeks, months, pass with the crime in hand on-going with other, every-day things, happening in the background. This inclusion of reality easily takes the reader to trudge alongside Constable Plank as he threads his way through the London streets of the 1820s, his steady tread always on the trail of bringing the lawbreakers to justice."
Helen Hollick of Discovering Diamonds book reviews

"The mystery at the heart of the novel is, as ever, beautifully explained and so meticulously detailed that nothing is ever left to chance and everything flows like the wheels of a well-oiled machine. There's an inherent dependability about Constable Plank which shines through in every novel and yet, I think that in *Faith, Hope and Trickery* we see an altogether more vulnerable Sam which is centred on Martha's unusual susceptibility and on his unerring need to protect her."
Jo at Jaffareadstoo

Praise for *Heir Apparent*

"Heir Apparent is possibly my favourite Sam Plank book yet, with great twists and turns to the plot and meticulous research. This author really gets the historical detail just right, but what stands out for me is the captivating character development the author has honed throughout the series, and I will own that for me the crime element is almost superfluous, as it is the characters who keep me coming back to these books."
Peggy-Dorothea Beydon, author

"There's an authenticity to the characters, particularly Sam and his wife Martha, which not only makes these stories such a joy to read, but which also gives such an imagined insight into life in the capital in the early 1800s so that it really does feel as though you are moving in tandem with Plank, Martha and the intrepid Wilson as they go about their business, forever trying, and usually succeeding, to live their lives in the full glare of the criminal fraternity."
Jo at Jaffareadstoo

Praise for *Notes of Change*

"I have followed this series from the start, and thoroughly enjoyed each and every one. Once again, the book immerses us in the streets of 1820s London, in the excellent company of constable Sam Plank and his wife Martha. This latest standalone case takes a number of well crafted turns, not least the reappearance of an old adversary in some unexpected circumstances, and all of which ties in nicely to the very apt title. A very worthy addition to the series and a very fitting finale."
Graham T, Amazon reviewer

"This well-written and thoroughly researched series strikes a balance between historical correctness and feel-good fiction – there's no hiding the harshness of life in Sam's era, but the warmth and depth of the central characters ensures they are comfort reads all the same."
Debbie, Amazon reviewer

LEARN MORE ABOUT GREGORY'S TIMES

Every month I produce a free e-newsletter featuring some of the research I have done on Regency times – from food and celebrations, to money and policing. Like most authors of historical fiction, I do far more research than I can ever use in my books, and it's all fascinating!

If you'd like to receive my free e-newsletter each month, please sign up at www.susangrossey.com/insider-updates

And as a little thank-you, you will receive **a FREE complete e-book of Fatal Forgery (the first book in the Sam Plank Mysteries series)** – and the chance to take part in occasional giveaways and competitions. See you there!

Made in United States
Troutdale, OR
07/27/2024